I0797059

THE GREAT GEORGIA DIRT DRAGON

THE GREAT GEORGIA DIRT DRAGON

J.S. PORTER

REJECT

THE REJECTED PUBLISHING GUILD

Identifiers:

Library of Congress Control Number: 2024911016

ISBN 979-8-9892038-3-3, print
ISBN 979-8-9892038-4-0, epub
ISBN 979-8-9892038-5-7, kindle

Cover photo by Herbert Santos. Cover design by J.S. Porter.

For Abigail

"All life feeds on life, each creature must yield its place in time to another, and at the heart of nature is a perpetual struggle to survive and increase at the expense of other beings. It is as if the entire cosmos were somehow predatory, a single great organism nourishing itself upon the death of everything to which it gives birth, creating and devouring all things with a terrible and impassive majesty."

DAVID BENTLEY HART
THE DOORS OF THE SEA

"He took a long snort and fell back on the seat, staring straight up at the sun. 'Turn up the fucking music!' he screamed. 'My heart feels like an alligator!'"

HUNTER S. THOMPSON
FEAR AND LOATHING IN LAS VEGAS

• • •

IN THE SUMMER OF 1991, my son was attacked and eaten by an alligator. He was four years old. I use the word eaten because no one else will. They say, "passed away." I am my son's mother. I, of all people, know he did not pass away—as if he evaporated peacefully and is somewhere else. The newspapers said "attacked" to avoid saying devoured. Same as when people say "passed away" instead of died. Like this helps. Like it's more delicate. What happened to Thad was not delicate, and I saw all of it. Several strong men had to drag me from the scene. They were practically shouting to be heard over my wailing. "He's gone," they were saying. "There's nothing you can do for him now."

Several months later, I had become obsessed with the deaths of small children. I sought out horrible articles and anecdotes about children who were starved or beaten to death, children that were flung through windshields in car crashes or who were crushed beneath vehicles in slow reverse. I knew things were getting worse when I started to dream about them. Like my mind—overflowing with dead kids—had nothing else to project on the blank screen of my subconscious, like a suitcase you can't close.

Then a man appeared at our door on a Saturday morning with a videotape.

It was uncharacteristically cold, an early fall in Georgia. The man was shivering, though likely at the sight of me and not the breeze of lapping daggers. My fragility casts a shadow of unease. This old man, his white-haired knuckles gripping the tape, trembling, squinting beneath gathered eyebrows, careful, like his gaze could topple me. Leland stood before me, a wall of mechanical chivalry and husbandly duty, his frame splayed to shield me from the world. I was scowling into the grey gnaw of autumn, distracted by the yellowed leaves on our lawn, the sheer number of them.

The man with the tape mentioned my son Thad.

After the man left, Leland had me by my shoulders—holding me up lest I collapse. He was saying the same boring things that had begun to ornament my every outburst and meltdown. "Stop it, Tessie," in his commanding baritone. "You have to stop this."

The man had decided not to turn his videotape over to the police because the attack had been witnessed plainly by several bystanders, myself included. There was no mystery as to what happened. "I reckoned best thing for everyone was to destroy the damned thing," he said, looking at the tape with hatred. "I sure am sorry to be here, ma'am. I reckon it wasn't my place. Thought real hard on it. Prayed on it. Cain't find no peace."

I cocked my head, birdlike when the man mentioned praying. For months I'd been hearing that "the Lord took Thad home." As if God were a savage reptile whose bloodlust made no distinction between soulless fish and little boys. Close friends would say this. Family. With their clammy hands on my shoulder, eyes wet: "The Lord took Thad home." And me, blinking slow, revealing the first of many troubling signs, I said, "God ate my son?"

Leland would not accept the man's tape. "It won't do any good, Tessie," he said. "It's not right, having that tape in our house."

The man's grandson played on Thad's tee-ball team.

That is how he came to record the incident. “I cain’t say why I kept recording,” he admitted, unable to look at us, probing the empty sockets of gums that once housed his young teeth. “I was petrified, you unnerstan? Then I s’pose I thought there might be some use for it if I could see where he up an’ went.”

“Where who went?” I said, breaking my silence.

The man looked down like a scolded child.

“The alligator? Or my son?”

“We sure appreciate your concern,” Leland interrupted. “We can’t take it.”

I roused. “Leland.” He raised an arm in front of me as if I were likely to charge. “Leland.”

The man saw me then. Not as a vessel of grief but as a woman caged by life and death. He was, I think, the first to see what had begun to grow behind my eyes. When he saw it, his face twisted. Leland reached for the door, my fingernails sinking in his forearm. My husband could not understand why I needed this tape. He was, like all the world, calling down to me from a ship I could not board. The tape belonged to a world he was leaving behind. I could leave with him if I would just ascend the ladder and board the ship. Leland had begun to resent my tarrying, needless and self-indulgent.

The Man with the Tape was the first omen of the fall. The second appeared about twelve hours later.

I'd wrapped myself in a blanket and sat coiled and crying on our couch, refusing Leland's halfhearted and begrudging efforts to console me. I realized that at some point I had begun to scratch at my ribs and back. I tried to picture what was on that tape, visualizing every frame of it, exaggerating each detail so that it became a carnival of horrors in my imagination. Ignoring my little episode, the TV went on reminding me about indestructible Timex watches, vacation possibilities at Epcot Center, *Curly Sue* coming to a theater near you. I'd calmed down when an ad for the season premiere of *The Wonder Years* reactivated my mania and I felt like a stone gargoyle had settled on my chest, mocking my shallow gasping for air.

When the gargoyle spoke, it was the voice of John Tesh. "Entertainment Tonight has the story for Tuesday, October 22, 1991."

Leland was asleep when I came to, the house somber and silent. Sleep had become for me like an orgasm, complicated and elusive, a release to chase without guarantee of capture, cat and mouse. The living room was cold, and I sat upright on the edge of the couch. If Leland had touched me in the last few weeks, he'd be surprised to find my bold ribs and joints beneath the silk wrap of my slip. Other women had always reproved of my smallness under the thin veneer of flattery, so it seemed fitting that when the Darkness set in, my lithe limbs became harsh, my thin and supple frame corrugated and angular.

I was aware of my breathing, inaudible beneath the dull whirl of a ceiling fan. I placed a trembling hand over my breast. The caged muscle fluttered within, a mocking thud.

I'm still here, there's more.

My once full breasts had been partially deflated by motherhood. It didn't seem fair, beauty. Though my body practically vibrated with need, I relished this chrysalis of agony—that Leland would not hold me, that friends could not bear to hold my gaze. This seemed fitting in a world where little boys are torn from their screaming mother's arms. Everything an ugly fucking block of ice.

I roved the silent house. Navigating an invisible

tightrope, sweeping each leg in a low arch as I paced, find the line, keep walking.

I'm still here, there's more.

I stood in the open doorway of the master bedroom, Leland's shape in the bed like a series of rocks. I ran my fingers down the shuttered panel doors of the hallway closet, tap tap tap. I approached the closed bedroom, sealed like a tomb, where hangs a crude drawing in crayon, little boy and woman, red hearts.

I returned to the living room where a lunar haze leaked from the French doors and into the den. I knew then that beyond the threshold, out in the backyard, it was waiting, black and ancient.

I opened the doors like a princess in a tower, and there it was. Under the canopy of stars, the scene scored by a symphony of crickets and cicadas, in the moonlit loam of our backyard, lay an alligator. In my heart I knew. It was him.

I'm still here. There's more.

7

THE CLOCK RADIO ERUPTS with what comes into focus as the second half of "Losing My Religion." Leland is gone for the day. I move my hand over his side of the bed, voided, cold to the touch. Shades drawn, the eggshell walls and beige carpet are dull with grey October dawn. The phone rings.

As if compelled, I return to the French doors. The backyard is empty. Beyond it, the work shed. Further still are sprawling acres of Savannah's wooded marshland. Maybe it's there now, amidst the murk and palmettos. The answering machine intervenes, records a dial tone. The phone rings again.

I answer, "hello?"

"Tessie," says the voice of my closest friend. "It's Ouida."

"I know."

"You didn't come in this morning."

"I was up all night."

"Are you okay? Are you sick?"

"Yes."

"I'll bring you something to eat."

"I have food, Ouida."

"Don't be bitchy. I know you have food. If you're sick, I'm going to bring you something. Are you sick?"

"Yes. Fine."

I can hear the decrescendo of her frustrated sigh as she lowers the phone to the receiver. I look back at the French doors.

Stepping outside, the grass is wet. A crystal thatch of frost encrusts the work shed's roof. I hug myself in a cold breeze, and a heron lands in front of me. "You're not him," I tell it.

Inside, I crawl under the long dresses in my closet and move a pile of shoes aside to reveal a gifted copy of *A Grief Observed* (which I did not read) and, tucked inside, a collection of library printouts and newspaper clippings.

"Infant Dies in Car Crash," reads one headline. "Body of Slain Two-Year-Old Discovered," another.

There's also "Hunt for Missing Child Continues" and "Parents Devastated by Tragic Loss." I sink into the closet, the hems of my dresses overhead becoming a pillow, and lift one newspaper clipping at a time. A little girl bludgeoned to death by foster parents, an infant stabbed twelve times, a baby toddler drowned in a swimming pool. I look at the monochromatic photos of these little faces, imperfect, ink smeared by my handling, and I attempt to imbibe their pain, the suffering of their loved ones. I think of every lull in my anguish over the last few months, moments when I felt little pain or nothing at all, distracted, numb, and I work to fill the empty cisterns of these moments with molten hurt.

Before all this, I was very happy.

At the Savannah Public Library, I found a book about Albert Fish, a nightmare man who did horrible things to children. I read about a four-year-old boy named Billy Gaffney. I did not borrow the book and bring it home for fear of Leland's disapproval, but I returned to its pages throughout lunch breaks during the crawl of my workdays. The passages that detailed the killing of Billy Gaffney induced a visceral reaction, something I felt in my stomach, a painful heat at my temples. What most haunted me about the story was not the unbearable details of the boy's torture and mutilation, nor even the fact that Fish claimed to have eaten him. What kept me from sleep for days after reading about Billy Gaffney was that before his death, he had been seen with his abductor on a Brooklyn streetcar. It was February, and Billy had no coat. He was crying for his mother.

Years ago, I attempted an openness with Leland in matters of morbid fascination. Leland, upright Southern man he is, did not think it "decent" to ponder death. Leland received the horrors of life as incumbent transactions. He stood in line and dutifully accepted each parcel issued by whatever forces governed his existence. If the parcel was good, he accepted it with grateful calm. If the parcel was evil, he managed the transaction in forbearing silence, filing it amongst other parcels in the seemingly endless compartments of his life.

For me, this arrangement was a messy one. All of life came to an anticipatory hush at the issue of a new package, and whatever happened after the package was opened had no choice but to bow before my *feeling* it. I would come undone with joy, and I was trampled by pain. Leland was forever misunderstanding this process as a weakness, an inability to bear up under a world poised to crush me. Whether he attributed this shortcoming to wiring or femininity, I couldn't say, but Leland was wrong. It didn't seem right to bypass *feeling* something, to ascribe some significance to all this, whether euphoria or despair or some overlap of both things. Feeling something, I thought, was not being overpowered by it. To file away the events of life seemed to me a fast-tracking of our insignificance. Aren't each of us, after all, helplessly marching toward erasure? All of us are powerless before the capricious savagery of life's distribution system. All of us line up with open hands until we are dead. Some of us receive these packages with resignation, organize them, line up again. Some of us make a mess, predisposed by a wicked world.

I'd forgotten the phone call with Ouida when she lets herself in. She's carrying a Styrofoam cup.

"What's that?"

"It's soup," she says, her eyes on the TV. "Why do white people love this show?"

I shrug. "Am I the ambassador for all white people? It's *Wings*. I don't know."

"It's just *Cheers* in an airport."

"So?"

"White people love *Cheers* too. Apparently, there are no black people on Nantucket," Ouida says, sitting down beside me, extending the cup in my direction.

"So go to Nantucket and fix it. What is this?"

"I told you it's soup. You *look* sick."

"Thanks." I pry open the plastic lid, a nauseating yellow plume of chicken broth wafts up. Ouida looks around.

"Does Leland know you called in?"

"Leland is not paying attention," I say, sipping the cup. "I didn't call in."

"No, you didn't. But I told Jerry you did. You know, that well of mercy will dry up."

I hadn't thought of my boss or what he'd think about me not showing up to work.

I tell Ouida, "I doubt Jerry is any more worried than I am about him finding some other woman to sit behind a desk and answer the phone."

"Tess," Ouida says.

"I didn't sign a contract in blood."

Ouida changes the channel. On the screen, Anita Hill is being grilled by a committee of senators. Holding the steaming cup to my face, I extend an index finger at the TV.

"She looks like you."

"Tess."

"Or you look like her."

"Who put pubic hair on my Coke?" Anita Hill says into a microphone.

I look at Ouida. She furrows her brow and says, "What's going on?"

I breathe deep, eyes on the TV, and settle back into the couch. "Nothing," I say. "Everything is going back to normal."

Leland's work truck returns at dusk. I watch from inside as he climbs out of the driver's seat, his pants streaked in the dark green of bleeding sod. Even from a distance, I can see the dirt gathered in his nail beds and in his creased brow. He rummages amongst the gas cans, weed eaters, and lawnmowers in his truck, moving a few items in and out of the work shed. When he steps inside the house he smells of sweat and grass clippings. I am drawn to this.

I wait like a fool while he showers, a silent beacon of need. When he emerges, dappled and steaming, something lurches inside me.

"How was work, baby?" he asks, pressing the towel to his face.

"Uneventful."

He snorts. "Ain't it always?"

"I don't want to be there anymore."

He looks at me for the first time that day. "You want to stay home?"

"I want something else."

To this, he offers a resigned chuckle. "Well, I'm not sure what jobs are out there for a pretty girl with a seminary degree. What do you want to be, a preacher?"

I consider his words. "No."

"I'm not sure how many Georgia boys would show up to hear a woman tell them what to do."

"Is that what a preacher does?" I smile. "They tell men what to do?"

He shrugs. "The ones any good at it."

He pinches my chin gently between his thumb and index finger. I try to somehow pass a message from my skin into his that I am not okay. He smiles and returns to the bathroom, closing the door behind him.

When Leland is asleep, I know before I look that the alligator will be back. When I see it, I think about the videotape that Leland kept from me. I wonder how he would describe it. *I protected her*, he'd say. Making awkward, furtive movements in the dark, I climb from the bed and creep down the hallway that connects our bedroom to the rest of the house. I arrive in the den with anticipation and looking through the glass panes of the French doors, observe what I somehow knew I would find there.

I open the French doors and the alligator shifts, moon reflecting in the black obsidian of its eyes. I make slow strides through the cold lawn, a chorus of insects hails my coming. Squatting in the grass a few feet from its glistening armor of scutes, I'm sure this is the one. This I can feel. I am chained to it. A lead ball of purpose grows in my brain.

. . .

Before all this, just months ago, I used to be someone who laughed. All my life, people told me my laugh was infectious, an airborne contagion that would crack the eggshell exterior of cold bystanders. My head would rock backward, sending my laughter toward the heavens like a prayer.

Leland was less generous with his laugh. He smirked, smiled with his eyes, grunted his approval. Making Leland laugh became a noteworthy accomplishment, something everyone who knew him well noticed and celebrated. Even then, it was usually little more than a deep and brief chuckle, if that. One Christmas ago, I'd written down the names of some tools Leland constantly bemoaned—the inadequacy of the ones at his disposal, his frugality crippling any motivation to replace them. I walked to a hardware store one cold afternoon in November, presented the list, nodded politely as the clerk condescended, making a fuss of the "pretty little lady in a hardware store" before the transaction was complete. I stowed the package in a closet, and Leland happened upon it a few days later.

Laughing hysterically, I climbed on his back as he playfully threatened to open the parcel before Christmas, pulling him backward, tears of laughter stinging my eyes, the ludicrousness of my weakness against his strength. Eventually, Leland agreed to honor the Christmas contract.

The next morning, the two of us sat on either side of our kitchen's island while it was still dark out. Us in our robes before steaming cups of coffee, Leland playfully pressed me about the gift.

"I could be using those tools right now," he said.

"That's true," I smiled, tilting my head in mock sympathy, my lips pouting for him.

"Give me *one* of them early."

"I'm sorry, baby. No."

He smiled, took a deep breath, and looked out the window.

Turning to me, he asked. "What if I die before Christmas?"

I sipped my coffee. "Then I'll return them."

Leland was quiet for a few seconds, then he threw his head back and bellowed a peal of deep laughter that filled the kitchen and the house as if he were a choir and our home a cathedral. I laughed too, hardly able to catch my breath, my stomach cramping from the work of it. The racket of our laughing woke Thad in his room, and this, too, was hilarious.

Thad wandered into the kitchen squinting sleep from his eyes, smiling at his strange parents.

"What?" he asked, giggling. "Why are you laughing?"

We gathered him, confused and smiling, in our arms and kissed his face.

I remember thinking then that this might be the closest things ever get to being perfect.

When we were newlyweds, we got a dog, Leland and me. The animal shelter was a predictably grime encrusted arrangement of concrete and cyclone fence. The animals all reacted to the two of us, desperate and pathetic, practically throwing themselves against their cages in the hopes of being released. There were mewling skeletal kittens with green mucus caked along their eyelids and drooling pit bulls. A fog of dejection hung in the air.

Blood spattered the painted brick of one dog cage. When I asked a volunteer what had happened, she called the phenomenon "happy tail."

"Dogs get so worked up every time people come in here. They want out so bad. They ain't got much space, so they wag them tails against that brick so hard the damn things bleed from it."

I said, "that's awful."

"It's a bitch to clean too."

I remember taking inventory of a conscious maternal urge then, a dormant bulb opening in my heart, to rescue an animal from this awful place, snatching it from the claws of death and sealing it away in the warmth of a loving home.

Leland and I locked eyes on a black lab, a puppy with a dopey, forlorn expression, it's smooth, dark coat iridescent beneath the ugly tube lights. The animal shelter became the entire world for me, mostly awful, peppered with the struggling bacteria of life. In my mind passed a hundred occasions of shameful indifference from my past when I beheld heartbreak and woe, frightened and overwhelmed, and did nothing. Maybe these kittens and pit bulls would be euthanized. Maybe no one was coming to rescue a million children being raised in loveless squalor, but I could take this dog home. I could mother it.

I wanted to name him Luther, and though Leland thought the name was too formal for a dog, he conceded to my begging, laughing on the way home as the puppy licked my face, shaking with excitement.

It was the three of us then. We referred to Luther as our son and we allowed part of our lives to revolve around his needs. The little puppy eventually became a clumsy, loping dog and we let him track mud through our living room, scolding him playfully. We let him sleep in our bed.

I remember thinking one night as Leland and I embraced this panting, stinking animal that we had opened the narrow borders of our interior world to make room for this other thing, and the glowing light that had only passed back and forth between Leland and me now spiraled around the three of us and I knew then that we could make a family.

When Thad came, Luther regarded this strange creature with fascination that gave way to affection. It was as if Luther could somehow intuit the baby's need for gentleness, for patience, and he bore the toddler's tugging at his tail and ears without yelping or biting or fleeing. Luther moved slow as Thad, oblivious to any discomfort he might be causing, made his arms a strangling wreath around Luther's neck. Luther seemed to step carefully so Thad would not fall.

Thad drew pictures of Luther. He let Luther lick his face. They chased each other in dizzying loops across our backyard. But then one day Thad was gone and only the dog was left. They say dogs know when to comfort grieving humans. When I would cry in the quiet darkness of my bedroom at night, Luther came to place his head on the mattress next to me and whimper. I would lay an open, lifeless palm on the smooth dome of the dog's head. That's what he was to me then. Just a dog.

• • •

The refrigerator bulb throws a cone of yellow glow over the white linoleum. I use a fingernail to puncture cellophane stretched over a mound of pink beef. A coppery-smelling droplet leaks from the opening and lands between my bare feet, a red sunburst of blood. I shuck the plastic from the meat like a sleeve of flesh and return to the back yard.

At first, the alligator seems uninterested or oblivious or both, but eventually pursues the trail of beef tendrils through the lawn and into the open French doors. Bringing it inside seems important, crucial even. It feels like this is the answer to a necessary question if I can just figure out how to ask it. With the alligator motionless on the living room carpet, I close the doors. It occurs to me that it has to go somewhere. Something inside me shuts down. The slow, disinterested blankness of the animal is disarming. I've become utilitarian, determined. Images of frenzied savagery forever tethered to this animal are, for the moment, evacuated from my consciousness. The animal is eight or nine feet long and so heavy that I discover I can't drag it by its tail, which is cold and dense, a leathery surface supple to the touch. It doesn't react in any way to me stepping over and around it, and if it weren't sluggishly lifting its head, it might seem dead. I'm very aware of any noise I'm making—the grunts and heavy breathing—and I frequently pause to listen for the bedroom door opening, but it never does. Standing over the alligator's back legs, I lean and nudge its side.

It stirs, crawling a few feet forward. I repeat my goading, and it lumbers into the hall, plodding heavily on the shag carpet. In the dark, I can see the white rectangle of paper still taped on the closed door where the alligator arrives. There I am in the drawing, a series of primitive bars and circles. A smaller stick figure—a little boy—is fastened to the jutting line of my arm. The inscription still reads: I love my mom.

So I put the alligator in Thad's room and close the door.

• • •

WHEN I WAS A little girl, Mr. Rodney was the local simpleton, and I saw the inside of his trailer only once. I'd been wandering from my front yard, ambling down the dirt road, swishing a thin branch in the air, the kind my dad used to fashion a disciplinary switch. A girl my age, vaguely familiar, appeared in the distance. The humidity of a Georgian summer had gone grey, the sky a murky soup of lead-colored rain clouds. The girl loped in my direction, her dirt-smudged face registering, a classmate of mine.

"I'm going to Mr. Arnim's store to git candy," she said, bypassing any formal greeting the way children often do. She opened her hand in the space between us, revealing damp quarters in her sweating grip, the lines of her palm caked in black. "You wanna walk down yonder with me? I can git you some candy too."

"Sure."

She talked as we went, unencumbered by the social hierarchy of the classroom. I considered her, noting her shoeless feet and distressed, ill-fitting t-shirt.

"Mama gave me quarters, but I cain't think of what I want to git. I don't like Snickers, and I don't want no gum or nothin' like 'at. I been wanderin' round out here 'cause I'm not s'posed to go back home yet."

"You could get a lot of little candy," I suggested.

"Like what?"

"Like those strawberry candies or lots of Bit-O-Honey."

"You like that stuff?"

I shrugged.

"I can git you some if you want, but *I* want somethin' chocolate."

I felt a jolt of irritation, then embarrassment. "I like chocolate too."

She leaned over to lift a rock, threw it. "But I like Skittles, too, though."

"Me too."

It seemed unkind to disagree with this girl who had, in her simple generosity, offered to buy me candy for no reason other than to purchase my company. She was renting me, and I wanted to be agreeable.

Crossing the threshold of his old store, Arnim eyed us over his glasses.

"Careful with them bare feet, sweetie," he said. "Don't you git no splinters, hear?"

The girl looked down at her feet, indignant. "I ain't gonna git no splinters," she said quietly, not looking at him.

The thin edge of tension between us peeled back as we argued playfully about candy, the purpose of wax lips, whether or not Nik-L-Nip tasted like medicine. In the end, we opted to share a Crunch bar, a bag of Skittles, and two small Bit-O-Honey pieces I felt too self-conscious to decline. Arnim counted the quarters by dragging them across his counter with a knotted, arthritic middle finger, finally releasing the candy to our care, and we went skipping out onto the store's creaking wooden porch.

I'd never befriended a neighborhood kid, someone I could access with a short walk. The prospect excited me. "I live just up the road," I blurted.

I watched as she worked a handful of Skittles in her filthy grip, then shoveled the entire helping into her mouth, some of them falling like bouncing pebbles on the floorboards below.

"I'm stayin' right there," she said, syrupy red saliva running down her chin. She pointed to a single wide trailer situated in the shadow of the store. "C'mon, my mama made some Kool-Aid." Without waiting, she bounded down the steps and toward the trailer, leaving me to catch up or flee, and I was needled by a twisting sensation that would not allow me to follow comfortably or decline, so I shuffled awkwardly behind her up to the white, linoleum-like refrigerator door of the trailer. A stale heat wafted out from inside, a smell like sweat and dust and rotting fruit. The melodramatic theme from *As the World Turns* blared from a tiny black-and-white TV, bent rabbit ears raised like a lifeless Jacob's ladder. A small boy, maybe six or seven years old, nude except for white briefs, his body a glistening sheen of sweat, rushed toward us.

"Didja git candy?" he asked, stringy hair sticking to his forehead.

"Mama said I ain't got to share it," the girl hissed.

"Nasty bitch," the little boy snarled, his hand in his underpants, scratching frantically.

Soiled dishes rose like sagging towers from the counters and sink, and the floor was nearly invisible beneath a landscape of molding TV dinner trays and mildewed laundry. A small foldout table rising from the center of the debris was strangely ornamented with oily machine parts. Behind a closed door rose the sound of a woman's voice, bleating and belabored, moaning, saying horrible, vulgar things I didn't understand but knew I wasn't supposed to hear.

The girl noticed my staring at the closed door, my shrinking at the woman's voice. "Mama's just in there havin' grown-up time with Mr. Rodney," she said, as if this cryptic reassurance was at all satisfying. "Like in the soaps when they kiss and undress and rub all over."

The boy leaned in and whispered in my ear, his breath hot and rank, "We tried it once."

I recoiled, reflexively wiping the warm damp of his voice from my ear.

The boy smiled, happy in his confession. "Me and my sister," he said, nodding at her.

"No we didn't!" the girl barked. The boy only rolled his eyes and looked at the TV, his mouth hanging open.

The girl sat in the mess without clearing a space,

tearing the Crunch bar from its wrapper and snapping it in two. "Here's your half," she said, extending the offering, her eyes caught in the tractor beam of the soap opera. I accepted the chocolate, squirming where I stood. "I probably need to go back home so my daddy don't get mad."

The door opened on the other side of the trailer, sweeping aside the garbage and wadded laundry with its swing. A large, sweat-beaded woman appeared wearing nothing but an oversized t-shirt and drooping white panties, her enormous hanging breasts bra-less and visible through the stretched fabric. Mr. Rodney followed behind her, buttoning his blue jeans. As the two adults moved carefully into the wreckage of the trailer's den, I could see into the bedroom where a baby, maybe a year old, peered over the edge of its crib.

"Sweetheart!" the woman squealed in delight. "You brought a little friend over to play?" She set her sights on me, a leering clown face, two front teeth missing from her brown smile.

"We got candy together, Mama," the girl said, lifting her half of the Crunch bar as proof of the event.

The woman put both hands over her mouth as if to

stifle a cry, her eyes welling. "My baby," she wheezed. "Sweetie," she said to me, "are you hungry? Why don't you stay for some supper?"

"I need to head home so my daddy isn't worried."

"We can call him!" she pleaded. "Arnim's got a phone in the store."

"I'm supposed to be home for supper."

The woman's face melted into a scowl, miserable and dejected. She looked to the girl who seemed frozen with humiliation. The baby wailed from the bedroom, everyone ignoring it. "She's rich," the little boy interrupted. "She's too precious to sit for supper with us."

The woman whirled around, eyes blazing, and growled at the boy through gritted teeth. "You shut your hateful mouth, you little shit."

"I ain't rich," I said.

"Hey, Tessie," Mr. Rodney purred.

"Y'all got Baby Thomas upset," the boy tisked, both hands scratching inside his briefs.

"Maybe you could come for supper tomorrow, sweetie?" the woman pleaded, her voice a desperate whine.

"I'd have to ask my parents."

"Let her go, Mama," the girl grunted, folding her arms. "She wants to go home."

"Thanks for the candy," I said to her, but she didn't look up. As I escaped the trailer, I could hear the woman scolding the boy. "You ran off our company with your hateful fucking mouth."

I could still hear the baby screaming when I turned on the dirt road and ran for home.

6

WHEN THE CLOCK CRIES out at 6 a.m. I stretch my legs into Leland's recently vacated side of the mattress and realize that I feel a simmering excitement, hear the dull and distant drums of panic. I stand for a few minutes outside of Thad's bedroom door. Something keeps me from opening it, so I take a long shower—the phone ringing the whole time—and for the first time in a long time, I shave and tweeze and exfoliate and shampoo and condition and moisturize and brush and put on something other than my short, salmon slip. I add foundation, eyeliner, mascara. I don't know why. By the time I've completed these feminine rituals, I feel hungry, but food itself seems strange and unappetizing.

The supermarket in our neighborhood seems like a pathetic place to demonstrate my mysterious surge of confidence, but I feel a pang in my stomach at the thought of venturing too far from home, and I'm still waiting for the pills to burn it away.

I smile at a young man sweeping leaves from the store's entrance. He says something I can't place.

"What was that?" I ask, fake smile stretching my face.

He leans forward. "Aren't you cold?"

He stares at my body, my short dress, bare arms and legs stinging from the chill.

"Oh," I laugh. "No, I'm fine."

He shrugs.

The interaction tampers my hunger, which, thirty minutes prior, seemed insatiable and is now little more than a distant whimper. Nothing seems good. I lift a can of soup and rock it back and forth, feeling the contents sludge to each side. I don't really want to buy a single can of soup (the act seems vulnerable, embarrassing), so I find a handful of ordinary groceries to disguise the can but can't shake the feeling that the cashier will see through my ruse.

"It's colder than I realized," I tell the cashier, laughing nervously. She smiles without looking up from a box of cereal. Heat gathers in my head as she takes the soup, pausing to find the barcode, and I realize I'm gasping like a small animal.

I am having some trouble.

"Did you know these are two for one?" she asks, brandishing the soup as if to mock me and my pathetic attempt to hide it.

"Excuse me?"

"The soup. You can get another one for free if you want."

I wave my hands around like I'm trying to silence applause. "Oh, I don't need two, thanks."

"You sure? You can go grab one if you want. Might as well. There's no one in line."

I look behind me, and suddenly the store seems desolate. I become convinced of an elaborate effort to trap me. I squint my eyes shut, wrinkle my nose, and take a deep breath.

"You okay?" the woman asks.

"Oh, I'm fine," I lie, exhaling. "Actually, I might be sick."

"Oh, no," the woman says in a baby voice. "You should bundle up!"

"I think you're right."

"Well, at least you have this." She stares at me.

"What?"

The smile vanishes, replaced by a mask of confusion. "The soup," she says, like it's a question, presenting the can I'd intended to hide.

I'm home for all of ten minutes when Ouida rings the doorbell. I can see myself, made up, reflecting in her glasses as she enters with a bewildered scowl.

"Are you going somewhere?"

"No."

"What's all this?" She waves a hand up and down my person like a magic wand.

"What?" I ask, annoyed, and suddenly embarrassed.

Ouida shakes her head, giving up. "If you were going to get all dressed up, why didn't you come to work? Jerry hit the ceiling."

"I'm not an administrative assistant, Ouida."

She puts her hand on her hip and shifts her weight to one leg, lowers her eyebrows. "You sure as hell have been acting like you are for forty hours a week over the last few years."

• • •

When I was a seminary student, I called myself Wheelchair. I felt like a special education student being wheeled in and out of "real" classes, drawing stares and embarrassed forced smiles like a sympathetic magnet. Men would approach me, grinning, child-like, and ask, "So what are *you* doing here?" They looked and spoke as if I were a cute puppy that had wandered into a classroom. I sat in stuffy rooms with no air conditioning, fanning myself with classwork, and the men would say, "It's getting too hot for Tessie," as if to juxtapose my weakness against their strength. Only the weak get uncomfortable. Only the weak experience temperature. Men spoke of "women" as if they were an issue to be resolved, quoting passages from the Bible about whores and head coverings, comparing women to alcohol ("a blessing and a curse"), to gambling ("permissible in moderation").

Beyond the tediousness of it, I didn't care. Nor did I feel any obligation to provide a satisfying explanation of my presence. I was, by disposition, upbeat and unfazed. I smiled. I laughed with and at my critics. The men postured like young CEOs, embellishing the size or difficulty of their ministries like they were measuring dicks. They were being sent out by influential denominations or staffed by sizable congregations. They rattled off bibliographies for their latest papers like industry credentials. My male classmates exuded an expectation of pronounced deference, as if the unbelievable fortune of my being there were owed to their tolerance of it. They seemed to expect polite apologies like I was forever crowding a grocery store aisle. They translated academic terms ad nauseam, as if I were lost, a bystander. When I was nearing graduation, one professor told me I was "too pretty" to go chasing after church work. He said I was gearing up to become the world's most overqualified Sunday school teacher. I blushed and demurred, somehow flattered and appalled in a single serving.

But I did not choose seminary to prove myself in a man's world. The truth was that I wasn't entirely sure what had drawn me to seminary, but one reason was probably my father.

I relocated four hours north from Savannah to Atlanta and drove home every few weeks. That no person in my life approved of or encouraged my decision—least of all my dad—only reinforced my resolve. I saw his face in every textbook, every Hebrew and Greek character, every haughty grin from my classmates and professors. I saw his gaunt cheekbones above his creased, sagging jowls, his hateful skull fixed to the bony column of his neck. I often thought of him rotating an apple against his pocketknife, explaining to me the ways of God, sweat beading on his upper lip in the muggy haze of summer.

He'd say, "Tessie, a holy God cannot tolerate sin in his presence. That is why he turns his face from the wicked. I'll be damned if he doesn't."

And I'd think, *Too bad for you, Dad.*

Damned indeed.

The Southern mind is a dark coil of zealous tribalism, at the center of which sits the heavy stone of loneliness. From birth, we are taught to draw lines around ourselves and the world, to recognize our interior world as good and to understand the world beyond our bubble as bad. We are hardened in tradition and inherited modes of hate, trained to affect a veneer of kindness we call "manners." God becomes a Southern Emperor who is as fretful and discriminating as we are and, thus, wholly unknowable.

We call this the fear of God.

With his adlibbed fire-and-brimstone sermonettes, our father would regale my sister Peyton and me with a half-balked theology of his own design.

"Daddy," Peyton asked him once, "since you know so much about God, why don't we go to church?"

"Because I don't serve a soft, silly man in a robe. I fear a righteous God."

Seminary, for me, was an organized effort to expose a fraud.

My mother said of my bachelor's degree, "But is all this *necessary,* Tessie?" I was drawing from a college fund appointed to me by my grandmother, but my mom often wondered aloud if "this seminary business" was what Nana had in mind. Of my graduate school decision, Mama could only sigh and echo the word in stunned disbelief. "Seminary?"

Mama had been robbed of what she felt was an owed lifestyle of the upper-class southern woman. Her parents had been wealthy and decent, but a daughter pregnant out of wedlock was enough for them to insist she marry my father, though he was decidedly below their station. The only thing worse than a poor son-in-law was a bastard grandchild. Daddy understood my mother's residual sophistication as a personal affront to his simplicity, and he punished her for it. Much of their parenting dynamic was a painful ripping and tearing at the awkward, infected seam of their union—a silken fabric of decency sewn haphazardly to the ugly burlap of self-righteous pauperdom. To endure the awful misfortune of a wife and children, my father, like most men of his generation, like his father before him, banished my mother from his inner world. My mother drank wine. They took to parenting as warfare, each of them navigating a tense civility, molding us like weapons for their incompatible ideologies.

On my decision to attend seminary, however, my parents were a uniform wall of disapproval. My father's first and final statement on the matter was to shake his head and say, "You won't find God there, Tessie."

The graduate school campus was a humble property ornamented with creaking wooden buildings likely funded and built by the elderly parishioners of a dying congregation. There were plaques to commemorate these people—names no one ever read or remembered. Even the campus chapel was "made possible" by the generous donations of such-and-such-who-cares.

Inside the chapel, six rows of pews faced an altar that almost always stood unoccupied. Students were encouraged to attend morning services, but I rarely did. I liked the chapel when it was empty, the diffused daylight piercing the darkness through panes of stained glass beneath a vaulted ceiling festooned with cobwebs. I spent hours alone in that chapel, the same arbitrary spot—third row, inside aisle. Facing forward, I would pray, read passages from my dog-eared Bible, and occasionally think about the skull of Saint Valentine.

I would imagine visiting Rome. In my mind, I would enter the Basilica of Saint Mary; with sweeping strides I moved along the concrete mosaics beneath, passing the ancient columns to the left side of the sanctuary where sits in an alcove carved into the stone wall the flower-crowned skull of Saint Valentine. The skull is inaccessible, roped off, blocked by votive stands to light silent prayer. Someone has labeled the skull. A garish white banner across the saint's braincase forever advertises S. VALENTINI M.

Death preserved in the place of prayer.

Other times I would visit in my mind the south of

France. I crossed the threshold of the Basilica of Mary Magdalene and made my way downstairs to the crypt. My palms sweating, a sense of strange dread in my stomach, I'd shuffle through the wet air and must until a glint of gold caught my eye. An elaborate reliquary peered back at me through an iron gate—four winged angels lifted the enormous golden head of Mary Magdalene, her face a hollow glass dome, like an astronaut's mask. Inside the mask lurks the ancient, copper-colored skull of Jesus's friend, leering and lonely in her crypt. They even keep an alleged fragment of miraculously preserved flesh in a vial beneath the elevated bust. The tissue was immortalized—the story goes—when it was touched by the risen Jesus.

Sitting in the quiet chapel, staring into an altar with no skulls or miracle flesh samples, I would touch my own arm, running my fingers along the soft skin and wonder what it was like to be loved so dearly that angels might lift up my remains for centuries. Years later, I thought of Thad's room.

Nearing graduation, I met Leland at a miniature golf course in Savannah while home one weekend in 1984.

My sister Peyton, now a high school junior, was clearly frustrated at being robbed the status of having a cool college sibling to instead endure small-town questions of my sanity. She loved me even so, this much was clear, and on a brisk February evening, she was obviously gathering the courage to ask me something.

"What, Peyton?" I challenged without looking up from my putt. I anticipated my father's indoctrination recapitulated by a helpless puppet. Instead, Peyton asked about God.

"Does the Bible really say that God can't look at sinners?"

Peyton couldn't bear to preface this question by acknowledging my qualifications to answer it. Such a thing would recognize some validity, however small, to my seminary debacle. The question itself was clearly a private one, as it was less about God or the Bible and more about our father.

I thought about giving Peyton a complicated academic answer. This might be my only opportunity to justify to her these last few years. But I didn't care if Peyton thought I was smart; I cared about purging our father's venom.

"The Bible doesn't say that" was all I said, and though lost in her own silent thoughts for the rest of the evening, this seemed to satisfy Peyton.

Our slow progress through the miniature golf course restricted the game of two boys playing behind us, who waited at a patient distance. When I offered to let them pass, Leland shook my hand and asked my name. I knew then.

He didn't really know what seminary was, but he said I looked like Lori Singer in *Footloose,* and though he was far from the first to point this out, I behaved as though he was. Men often did this, told me I reminded them of some famous actress or model known for her beauty or body, a means of extending an unspoken compliment, testing the waters. My girlfriends hated this and wanted me to have the decency to hate it with them, but I pretended to misunderstand it. When Leland compared me to Lori Singer, I shifted my weight to one leg and smiled. I let him get to third base on our first date, and we got married that winter.

1984 was a warm current of infatuation. Movie tickets were cheap, the darkness of the theater reliable, so we saw everything. He tolerated *Romancing the Stone* and

Splash, and I endured *Children of the Corn* and *Friday the 13th: The Final Chapter* with my face buried in his shoulder. Once, after sex in Leland's car, he said to me, "Bet you didn't learn to talk like that in seminary." He looked like my classmates then, dirty and smug, and my bubble of ecstasy was lanced by shame. Isn't all of love a wild oscillation between felt things?

I talked about the final months of seminary like they were a silly chore rather than a psychological triumph, and Leland would only nod, dismissive. I feigned indifference to my own graduation ceremony and the fact that Leland had not mentioned attending it. Afterward, I cried in a school bathroom, furious with myself, then laughed as something occurred to me. The shortest verse in the English translation of the Bible is John 11:35: "Jesus wept."

In the original language, the line is more like, "Jesus shed tears," but why say something with three words when you can say it with two? And anyway, there I was, just like Jesus.

I drove home from Atlanta to Savannah, arriving late. Leland was waiting on my parent's porch. He asked, "How was your day?" the specificity of its events without value.

"It was fine," I said, already warming to his proximity.

He knelt, produced a ring. I thought, this is the reward for my suffering, my seminary degree already wilting in the heat on the dash of my car.

Leland was a heavy man, heavy in his sturdy, tree-like build and heavy in his dignified stoicism. I felt like a doll in his arms, like we were one of those cartoon caricatures of a muscle man cradling a diminutive lady admirer with balloon breasts and hearts for eyes. During our brief courtship and through the early years of our marriage, Leland would sometimes drift in silent reflection, then muse about God. One humid summer evening, we sat in Forsyth Park, newlyweds, amber streetlamps reflecting in the nearby fountain's rippling pool.

Leland said, "God sure is mysterious."

I was, I remember, suddenly afraid.

"What do you mean?" I asked, leaning forward, unable to meet his gaze.

He seemed to wash up some place on the tide of this reverie. His face indicated he didn't like where he'd arrived, but the spell broke, and he turned to me with a fatherly smile, wrapping his big arm around me and giving my shoulder a gentle squeeze, as if this were an answer.

I wanted to tell Leland about my impressive bibliography of seminary research. About Augustine and John Calvin and John Wesley and terms like "Pauline Corpus" and "Abrahamic Covenant." I wanted to be an impressive little treasure trove of mostly useless information, an encyclopedia for him to reference and admire. I wanted to file a few light-hearted complaints about the amount of required reading on Ignatius of Loyola the way I'd overheard other students do in conversations to which I was not invited. I wanted to tell Leland that this petite, effervescent woman who had made for him such an agreeable wife had in her a rebellious streak. A defiant air. Maybe he'd be impressed by my paper on Jonathan Edwards, *Sinners in the Hands of an Abusive God: A Theological Critique of Edwards' Sociopathic Deity*, for which I'd been reprimanded and forced to revise "with respect." This same offended professor had argued that Martin Luther King, Jr. ought to be disqualified from pastoral respect due to his extramarital affairs. I'd spoken up, "What about King David?" The professor sighed, looked over his glasses to where I sat.

"David," I said again. "Because of the Bathsheba thing. No longer eligible for pastoral respect, right?"

The classroom, all men, made zero effort to disguise their theatrical exhaustion with my pushback. I didn't care.

When one of the few female faculty members invited me into her office to discuss an inch of my visible cleavage, I could only shrug.

"Tessie, are you dressing with consideration for your brothers in Christ? Do you want to become a stumbling block to them?"

"Because of this?" I asked, baffled, pointing to the offending cleft. "Isn't just having breasts at all still an issue?" I gestured at my chest, making two big circles with my hands. She averted her eyes, terrified she might contract my indecency, like if she weren't careful, we'd be gathered around the warm glow of our burning bras before she realized what happened.

Surely this story should amuse Leland, like discovering your favorite book has additional chapters you've somehow overlooked. Maybe he would cover his mouth the way he does when he thinks he might laugh. If he would just ask me about this unseen dimension of my person, stored away but living, bunked in a faculty of my skull.

Instead, God remained mysterious that night in Forsyth Park. My father's words in the warm, sticky breeze, "You won't find God there, Tessie."

The Tessie that Leland knew, he loved well, as best as he knew how. We were friends. We rented a studio apartment in January of 1985 and put a mattress on the floor. Leland's dad offered to exploit connections and secure for me an office job for the county board of education. I accepted. Leland carried on in his father's landscaping business. My seminary debacle accomplished, I pushed papers in a happy, floating stasis. I bought groceries after work and made Leland's dinner. We walked our labrador, Luther, on warm, humid evenings when the sun was still bright after supper. We bought a customized Christmas ornament with three names, Leland, Tessie, and Luther. We argued, playfully, about whether to watch *Who's the Boss?* or *The A-Team*. We laughed, had satisfyingly routine sex, shared ice cream from the same tub.

Two years later, I was pregnant.

Thad was conceived during a storm. Hurricane Charlie encroaching, electric filaments snaking across the black sheet of night, flashes of white casting long shadows in the dark apartment. The condom unopened on the nightstand when I asked Leland: "Don't put it on?" and he nodded in happy comprehension. Heavy in his way.

I was waiting in line. Somewhere up the shelf of my life, God was waiting to hand me life and then death. Always in that order.

. . .

Ouida goes through the house, turning on all the lights, grumbling to herself the way a mother does while cleaning up after a toddler. I lay on the couch watching *Wings* as if oblivious to her constant back-and-forth. She disappears for a moment, then remerges as a floating head gripping the door frame, her body in the hall.

"Has the dog been in here?"

"No," I grunt. Luther had been mostly relegated to the outside world for weeks. He wandered the backyard, the garage, or the work shed where Leland had built him a doghouse. I don't think either of us could bear to look at him.

"Well, did someone go in Thad's room?" Ouida presses.

I think for a moment about telling Ouida everything, realizing she might open the door either way, and I realize with some relief that I don't really care. I'm less anxious than I've been in weeks. Months.

"I don't know," I tell her. "No?"

"There's dirt all in the hallway and up to his door. The carpet's a mess."

I sigh, not taking my eyes from the TV. "Leland is usually filthy when he gets home."

Ouida goes on staring at me, the side of her mouth screwed up, then returns to her assessment of the hallway. I can hear her talking in there, but I assume it isn't for me. When she keeps at it, I finally half-yell, "Ouida, you know I can't hear you in there."

She appears. "Then turn off the damn TV, Tess."

"Just don't talk to me from the hallway."

"I want you and Leland to come out and eat with me and Lucius tonight."

"No, Ouida. Let's just eat here."

"Why?" She sits down on the couch, body turned to me, and touches my face like she's a doctor examining me for signs of fever.

I swat at her hand, a pestering fly. "Ouida, I don't like being dinner theater for the restaurant patrons of Savannah. I don't feel like being the amazing and offensive mixed-race double date tonight. Let them entertain themselves." Ouida fake-coughs, makes a face.

"What?" I ask.

"So, you care about this now?"

"I'm tired."

"You *look* tired."

"Thank you, Ouida."

"We're going out tonight."

"I'll ask Leland."

"Get up," she sighs, standing. "Let's go to work."

I throw my head back in exaggerated frustration. "Fine."

. . .

I loved taking Thad to restaurants. The sight of him, dwarfed by the tables and booths and silverware, giddied by the strangeness of it all—strange people bringing strange food to a strange table just because we told them to do it. Kicking his little legs from atop his booster seat, Thad would clench his fists in anticipation of the salad crackers that I would unwrap and dole out like candies while Leland challenged Thad in ridiculous sessions of Twenty Questions.

"Guess, Dada!"

"You have to give me a hint, Thaddy."

"It's a alligator."

"That's not a hint. That's the answer!"

"Okay, it's a big green animal with big sharp teeth."

"But now I know it's an alligator because you told me so already."

And Thad would laugh and laugh, endlessly amused by his ability to "stump" his father before the game had begun. I watched the two of them, the way Leland would lean over, inches from Thad's smiling face. Someone else might have assumed it was so that Leland could hear Thad over the din of the busy restaurant, but I knew the truth, he could hear just fine. It was to be close to him, so stirred by his love that he would wrap his arms around Thad and shake him in theatrical frustration.

"You're too good at this game! No fair!"

I would sit, elbow on the table, my chin in my hand, and watch the two of them, seeing Leland's face in Thad, the adoration on it as he peered up at this man who protected him, who could do him no wrong.

• • •

I smile through each of my coworker's careful greetings, welcoming me back after a day's absence as if I were a sick child. Ouida goes before me, shooing condescending coddlers from my path, saying, "All right people, she wasn't in the hospital, let's get back to work."

My desk is like returning to a disheveled storage unit. Stacks of papers, a bundle of multi-colored floppy disks hastily bound by a tangled rubber band, a spring-loaded pen that was left extended and, I'm sure, no longer writes. I sit, making a sound like a deflating balloon, and power up a sluggish IBM. I test the pen. It doesn't work.

A voice startles me. "You hear they're thinking about moving us to year-round schedule?"

I look over to see Gayle, her dark hair pulled back taut, making her otherwise perfect face look like stretched elastic. "What?" I ask.

"I heard Jerry talking about it yesterday. The board wants to move the entire county to the year-round school schedule. No summer."

"Who says?" asks Ouida's voice from my other side.

"I just told you," Gayle says. "Jerry. Our boss. I heard him say it myself."

"What does that even mean?" I ask, peeling the rubber band back from the bundle of floppy discs, which erupt from their bonds like a party favor, tumbling from my desk and on to the floor. No one acknowledges this.

"Well, *technically*," Gayle says, making air quotes, "the kids will still be in school for the 180 days, but there's no summer break. They just take lots of short breaks all throughout the year."

"Why did you need air quotes for 'technically'?" I ask.

"Parents are going to raise Cain," Ouida says, shaking her head.

"I'll tell you right now mine won't have it," Gayle snorts, crossing her arms and looking out into the office as if the place itself is her problem. "They will show their behinds, and I won't be able to blame them for it either."

I grunt, roving my desk for a new pen. "So what are you going to do about it, Gayle? We work for the board of education, we're not on it."

"I'm sure as hell going to say something, I can tell you that right now."

"Did Jerry say why?" Ouida asks.

"The superintendent is up his ass," Gayle begins, then looks around, leans over me, closer to Ouida, and whispers, "…up his *ass* about low test scores."

"You'd already said ass," I point out. "Whispering it a second time doesn't really help."

"So how is year-round going to change test scores?" Ouida scoffs.

Gayle lifts her hands in resignation and makes a stupid face. "Apparently, some studies show the kids remember more this way. Score higher."

Gayle sighs and scratches at her black nylons, the heel of her pump detached from her foot like the open mouth of a puppet.

"Parents are going to raise Cain," Ouida says again.

"I'm going to raise Cain," Gayle snorts. "And I'll just go ahead and say mine will lose their minds. My oldest is having a hard enough time as it is."

I'm gathering up my fallen discs when Gayle pats my back and says, "Sweetie? How're we doing? Y'all doin' okay?"

I dump the discs on the desktop and say, "One day at a time."

The only open table at Sizzler is a few feet from the grill, and two employees have decided to have an argument outside of the kitchen and within earshot of patrons, though no one seems remotely interested or concerned.

"Do you hear this?" I ask Ouida without taking my eyes from the confrontation.

"Why do you sound tired?" she asks. Ouida leans in and whispers, "Did you take those drugs?"

I roll my eyes. "It's called alprazolam. It's not *drugs*. It treats *bereavement-related disorders*." I make air quotes to invalidate the term, rolling my eyes at it.

"It makes you slow is what it does."

Across the table, Leland engages Lucius in their old argument about *Predator 2*.

"You look just like him," Leland is saying.

"Do all black people look the same to you, Leland?" Lucius asks, looking around the restaurant.

"Not all of them. But you look like Danny Glover."

"Look at my hairline, Leland."

"What about it?"

Lucius mimes a triangle over his scalp. "Does this look like a receding widow's peak to you?"

"A what? Like Dracula?"

"Like Danny Glover."

I'm absolutely flabbergasted by the mounting hostility between one guy in a hairnet, and another in, of all things, a tall chef's hat. Chef's Hat Guy brandishes a plate at Hairnet Guy.

"Then what is this?" Chef's Hat Guy says. "Huh? Nathan? Am I crazy? *What is this?*"

Hairnet Guy doesn't make eye contact. Shakes his head at the floor. An obese woman with feathered bangs pretends not to notice their arguing—or does and doesn't care—and calls out over the crackling grill, "Excuse me, when will there be more steak?"

Chef's Hat Guy tells Hairnet Guy, "Just go get Davey."

"Leland," Ouida says, using a fork to sort through a salad like she's lost something in it. "Have you been taking care of Tessie while she's sick?"

Leland looks at Ouida, then me. "I didn't realize you were sick."

I wave my hand like a ping-pong paddle. "It's nothing. Ouida just hates when I miss work."

Ouida grunts her disapproval. "You better make sure she's up in the morning if it's nothing," she tells Leland, like I'm not sitting right here.

I poke her arm with two fingers. "I have an alarm clock, Ouida. I wasn't feeling good."

Leland mistakes this as a coded reference to grief and nods solemnly, saying, "We're taking it one day at a time, aren't we?" I sigh and sink in the booth, my thighs squeaking on the vinyl upholstery. Leland returns to his crucial discussion.

"It's not an insult to be compared to Danny Glover."

"I didn't say it was," says Lucius, mouth full of a

questionable-looking steak. "I just don't look like him."

"Danny Glover beat the Predator. They gave him an old gun and everything."

"Right," Lucius rolls his eyes. "Arnold Schwarzenegger's whole team of special-ops bad-asses gets wiped out by this thing, Arnold escapes within an inch of his life, but Danny Glover kicks its ass? Give me a break."

"Ouida," Leland says, "doesn't Lucius look like Danny Glover?"

"Listen," I interrupt, eyes wide. "Do you hear this?" I lift an index finger and nod to the beat of "Losing My Religion," playing somewhere in the distance.

"What?" Ouida asks.

The song ends. Karyn White's "Romantic" replaces it. "You missed it," I sigh. No one cares.

I take an inventory of myself, looking for some sense of what I realize should be discontent with the evening. The alprazolam is making me distant. I'm like a researcher in a lab coat, dutifully cataloging a series of justifiable emotions and reactions without touching them. I'm not allowed to touch them.

Standing in the Sizzler parking lot, I feel colder than I should, my eroding layer of body fat making me vulnerable. I hug myself and sidle up beside Leland as we say our goodbyes, my jutting elbows raking against the xylophone ribs beneath my dress. I press myself into Leland's side as if I am a fitted piece missing from his arrangement. He puts his arm around me, but it's a display gesture, unburdened by emotion. Husband embraces wife. We are taking it one day at a time.

At home, Leland has locked himself in the bathroom when I begin to undress. Half-naked, I pause, listening for evidence of his imminent return. When the bathroom door opens, I continue undressing, hoping to agitate him with lust or worry or both. When he sees me, he stops, looks away. "Sorry," he says, retreating. This man that has known my body in ways more intimate than even me now turns his face from it. The last lingering wisps of alprazolam fog lifting, I raise my arms, thread them through the spaghetti straps of my pink slip, skin dimpling at the prick of cold air, a colder October than usual.

I get out of bed just before 1 a.m. Leland seems

thoroughly mired in sleep. When I draw up the bedroom's window shades, I can see his eyes struggling beneath their lids, two cats trapped under blankets.

I creep down the hallway, eyes shut, tiptoeing into the dark kitchen and rocking the television dials so that the electric hum stirs the silent air around me. On the screen, a pair of lithe hands with long painted nails move with mime-like theatricality around a bottle of perfume.

"And ladies," a disembodied voice says, "your husbands are going to love this perfume. Again, this is *Dune* by Christian Dior, and this feminine scent possesses a blend of amber and wallflower as well as watery notes of the fresh, cool sea air. We recommend this for daytime wear, ladies. It is going to drive your husbands crazy."

The onscreen text indicates that while the perfume retails at $36, it has been discounted to half as much. I mouth some of the words I've just heard, "amber, wallflower, sea air." This seems important.

A man answers my call—not the flowery-sounding hostess on the TV—and wants to take my order.

"Yeah," I say. "Is there any way I can go on the air? I

want to talk to the lady selling the perfume."

"I can actually take your order here, ma'am."

"Well, I know, but who ends up on the actual show?"

"I beg your pardon?"

"Like, how do you choose who to push through to the show?"

"Oh, I don't make those decisions, ma'am, but I can take your order here."

"Where is here?"

"Ma'am?"

"Where are you right now?"

"I'm at my desk, ma'am."

"I work at a desk," I say.

"And you want to order the perfume?"

"Have you smelled it?"

"The perfume?"

"Yeah, is there some there? Can you tell me if it really smells like amber and wallflower and sea air?"

"I don't have any of the perfume here, no, ma'am."

"I guess I don't really see how it could smell like all those things."

"I didn't know wallflower was a real flower," he admits. "I thought it was an expression."

"I don't know," I say, taking a deep breath. "My husband used to love it when I wore perfume."

It's quiet for a moment. "I'm sure he'd love this perfume," the man says.

"Maybe."

I catch myself falling asleep at the counter, the woman's patronizing voice like a lullaby. I drink a Folgers Coffee Single, wincing at the bitterness of it, and force myself to stand up. At first, all of my movements are surgical and exhausting for fear of waking Leland, but when I drop a spoon that clangs comically on the counter and floor, I decide I don't really care.

In the hallway, there's a smell, faint and tidal, like fish and the washed-up exoskeletons of dead crabs. I see the mess Ouida mentioned, and I'm surprised that Leland, who is usually very concerned with indoor cleanliness, overlooked it. There are broad, blackish streaks, like burns in the carpet. There's a flash in my brain, a jolt. The thought is a dentist's pick probing the rotted cavity of my memory. I can see a snapshot through the painful portal of time: Thad's muddy footprints by the French doors. I tense, push the thought away, and open the door to Thad's bedroom.

The contents of the room move out from the door in a staggering reaction-inducing shockwave, and I have to brace myself against the doorframe to stave off collapse. I'm being trampled by it, the overload of memory and felt things. I cover my mouth so I won't scream or vomit or call for Leland.

The things that affect me most: Thad's clothes by his bed, which I removed when I dressed him in his tee ball uniform three months prior, his final moments in our house. The smell of marsh and death. The alligator that ate my son. It uses stubby arms to shift its bulk and face me where I stand, its foul presence in this sacred place a desecration of my own shambling design. It occurs to me that I am sitting.

"Hard to keep standing," says the alligator.

I cinch my eyes shut, hand still over my mouth, and give in to a series of bodily tremors.

"Do you want to go somewhere else?" it asks, its voice all gravel and gutter.

My eyes still closed, I nod my head yes.

The air is suddenly muggy. I flinch at the explosion of layered white noise, the din of frogs and insects.

Drawing my hands from the stab of grass, I convulse and throw up. Drooling, ropes of bile and Sizzler house salad hanging from my chin, I think to ask, "Where are we?"

"Hatching of Ruben," comes the voice of the alligator beside me.

I become aware of a mound beside me. All wet dirt and sodden twigs, roughly the same size and shape of my hunched frame. I am on the bank of a river. It's dark except for the white glow of a full moon. Another alligator moves through the water like fluid through a winding tube. Approaching the mound, the swimming reptile triggers a cacophony from inside of what sounds like video game laser blasts. The squeaking hatchlings, a scurrying avalanche of black scales and zigzagging yellow stripes rush to the water and surround their mother. The phenomenon is soulless—a biological mechanism, the cosmic cellular-level clockwork of primordial motherhood.

A heron bobs on the periphery, behind the nest, observing the water's activity from a distance. Several writhing alligator infants struggle in the mound's debris, little limbs a paddling work of futility. The heron cocks its head at the stragglers, and with a few stabbing gulps, seizes them in its beak, shaking them violently loose from the connectedness of their skeletons. It feeds on their squirming bodies, then strides from the nest, satisfied.

"Why are we here?" I ask.

"Me," the alligator answers. "Born into death."

It moves its slow head to the scene of recent slaughter. A hatchling remains, injured, but spared from the heron's gullet.

"This is you?" I ask.

"Ruben," says Ruben.

My ankles burn from squatting. I sit down in the grass, tired, and lean back against Thad's bed.

I'm back inside.

I take a deep breath of central heating. The smooth, supple flesh of Ruben's tail moves along my thigh as he shifts in place, and I shiver. It occurs to me that my hand is in Thad's t-shirt, and before I can come to my senses, I lift it to my face and inhale. Death preserved in a place of prayer.

I keep the shirt to my face to muffle my weeping. Jesus shed tears.

Ruben uses his back legs to lift his hips from the carpet. An orifice distends from the base of his tail, and a pool of watery shit empties from his bowels and over the rest of Thad's little outfit, never to be worn again.

. . .

I was not an idiot about our love. I knew that the burst dam of our infatuation for one another—the smothering of one another with whispered adoration like bad poetry, the frantic pawing at and exploring of one another's bodies that gave way to hungry fucking—I knew that it would evolve. I wanted to marry Leland anyway.

I savored our season of new love, anticipating the next season of domesticated calm with a kind of smiling curiosity. What would we be like as happy friends, as content to sit together over breakfast as we were thrashing our bodies together in a heightened state of melting intimacy? The new season came like autumn and settled over us, welcoming and homey. Two years later, I realized I had been bleeding something out, like I had adjusted to the discomfort of an unknown ailment only to lift my shirt and discover an open wound, wet and red, yawning open like a fish gasping for air.

Leland's love had shapeshifted. It was there, often familiar, but it had adopted new moods and methods I did not anticipate. Leland no longer touched, he only touched back. His kind words, once warmly routine, shriveled to nothing, the pleasantries of an acquaintance. Other people—other *men*—would sometimes compliment me, tell me I was beautiful, and I would relay this to Leland, hoping to stir some dormant jealousy in the subconsciousness of his love. He would only nod as if this was as nice and as uninteresting a detail as a comment on traffic patterns or the weather.

Finally, practically shivering in the cold of my loneliness, I would ask Leland what had changed. Was it me? Him? Someone else? He was exasperated then, angry and defensive, at the end of his rope with this clamoring heap of desperation pulling at his pant leg like a shameless beggar. He did so much, he would sigh, exhausted; nothing was ever enough for the greedy black vortex of my need. Confused, I would acquiesce, limping back to the corner of my sadness, carefully assessing the infectious wound, and wondering if I put it there or if he did.

For a while, I hated myself for wanting him so badly that I could starve for his love. On other days though, I would think: fuck Leland.

Then the sun would rise, and I would no longer find that hungry version of myself, nor the cold stone Leland that I was sure had devoured the old one. He held me, and I held him back. It was as if, while down in the abyss, I saw a dangling cord of rescue, and I reached out my skeleton and grabbed it.

When the sun shone brightly on our love—on our good days and in our right minds—we had both agreed that Thad would be an only child. Though he often asked for a brother, and though neither of us had discussed or planned to remain a family of three, we discovered one evening as we talked that we liked things the way they were and saw no reason to change them.

"Just the three of us," Leland winked at me.

"Just the three of us," I smiled, unable to help myself.

...

Back in the bedroom, Leland stirs at my attempt to return undetected.

"Tess?" he says, leaning up on an elbow. In the haze of sleep, he's become uninhibited, forgetting everything awful and broken, he draws my body up to his. I can feel his familiar heat against my hip. My heart races.

"Maybe we should make another one," he says, his beard on my cheek. "Remember how Thad wanted a brother?"

My thawing heart freezes over in an instant.

"Thad is dead," I say, nearly choking on the words. My husband withdraws his embrace and returns to his side of the bed, the space between us crowded with misery.

• • •

DURING THE SUMMERS OF my childhood, my mother would occasionally leave my sister Peyton and me with her old friend when she had errands to run. Spoiled by the freedom afforded her while my sister and I were in school, she'd say, "I have things I need to get done, and I can't do them with you two girls clawing at me and each other all damn day."

The pear-shaped babysitter with grey bouffant hair we knew only as "Miss Tois." She haunted an enormous, rickety-looking household my mom described as being "as old as Georgia itself." Several local parents would pay Miss Tois a nominal honorarium in exchange for a few hours' peace on long summer days when it was too hot to think straight, let alone corral bored and whining children.

When I was ten, Peyton and I visited Miss Tois once every week or so, but there were two boys that, as far as we could tell, spent every day with her. One of them was Holt, an angular spider-like thing who mostly operated the other, Cole, several years his stubby junior. Emboldened by their significant tenure, the two brothers roved the old house at will, exploring its secret chambers like the faculties of a massive skull. I didn't like Miss Tois or her strange, creaking manor, but Peyton loathed these visits, fastening herself to my side as if the house itself might swallow her if she wandered off on her own. Whenever my sister and I crossed the threshold of the old house, Holt and Cole came scrambling, seeking us out like dogs catching a scent.

"Do yah think yer pretty?" Holt asked me one scalding, sticky afternoon as the four of us wandered the house's perimeter. He took great whooshing swats at the overgrown grass with a thin stick that cut the air like a whip.

"I don't know."

"She *is* pretty," Peyton said.

"Well, who the hell asked you?" Holt snapped, leveling the stick at her as if he could shoot her with it.

Looking back at me, Holt said, "I'll give yah a nickel if you show me yer pussy."

"No."

"Stop it, Holt. They'll git you in trouble," Cole warned.

"Let us see for just five seconds," Holt pressed. "I'll count fast."

"I don't wanna see it," Cole said, afraid.

Squinting one eye, Holt hovered the stick point in the air over my crotch. "My daddy said women jist use their pussies like weapons to git men by the peckers and control 'em."

Peyton looked up at me. I knew she was confused but too afraid or embarrassed to ask for an explanation. I swatted the stick away. "I'm going to tell Miss Tois what you're saying if you don't stop it."

He turned, drawing something in the air with his stick and said, "Bitch."

Peyton threaded her fingers through mine, her palm clammy with sweat.

The four of us moved further into the mossy canopy of wooded acreage that surrounded the house until we heard the pathetic mewling of an animal.

"What's that?" Peyton whispered up at me.

"Miss Tois has a shitty old hound chained up out

here," Holt said, still walking and pointing with his stick.

In the shade of a sprawling oak rose a tumbledown shed. There, in a bald clearing sat a shivering dog, a length of chain looped around its neck for lack of any collar, tethering it a cruel three-foot distance from an iron stake. The dog was patchy and red, its flesh a rutted topography of open sores. Practically convulsing at the sight of us, a thin, snaking trail of urine appeared beneath the dog, crawling out across the packed dirt and gathering in a dusty little pool.

"S'wrong with it?" Peyton asked.

"Got mange," said Holt. "Heard Tois say it's got some kinda pest. Like chiggers, but they dig up under yer skin and eat ya from the inside."

"How come ain't nobody helpin' it?"

"Nobody wants to touch that shitty old thing."

"Where's its food?" I ask, observing the emaciated animal's heaving ribcage.

"Shit fire," Holt groaned, pinching his nose. "Smells like its dead already." He inched forward, grimacing, and extended the stick until it poked one of the dog's angry red lesions. The dog yelped, and the four of us recoiled, shocked by the urgency of it.

"Leave it alone," I said.

"It ain't like it can git any worse," he shrugged, spitting. "My daddy said they ought to shoot it. We had us a shitty old mutt once. Damn thing was always pregnant. Cole and me had to drown most of them pups out yonder in the pond."

"You drowned the pups?" Peyton asked, her nervous fingers in her mouth.

"Hell yeah, we drowned 'em. Din't we, Cole?"

Cole frowned at his feet and kicked a rock.

Holt went on. "Damn things can swim too, even when they's little. What we did was put 'em in a hen cage, tied a rope 'round it, and threw that fucker out into the pond. Cage sank like a stone, them pups just raising Cain as they went on down."

"You just left them down there?" I asked.

"Nah, we needed us that cage. Cole and me, we just waited a few minutes and hauled it back up. Sure enough, all them pups was deader'n shit in there 'cept one of 'em. It just took to coughin' and pukin' its guts up."

"Did you bury 'em?" Peyton asked, barely audible.

"Didn't yah hear me?" Holt snapped. "We did that with damn near every pup the ol' bitch popped out. I ain't bout to bury litter after litter o' mutts in my backyard. We dumped them sorry ol' things out in the marsh, let the gators and snappin' turtles get at 'em."

"What happened to the mama?"

"My daddy got sick of us drowning them pups and finally put the ol' bitch down." Holt leveled an imaginary gun at the sore-ridden dog and mimed a blast. "That ol' thing got shot once and popped right back up. Went to runnin' round our property with half its head hangin' off, I swear to God. Daddy had to chase it around, just hootin' and hollerin'. Boy, me and Cole like to die laughin', didn't we Cole?"

"I didn't laugh," Cole mumbled.

"Anyway, that sorry old dog was miserable anyway. We forgot to even feed it half the time. Better for it to be dead."

We stared at the dog for a silent moment.

"They ought to shoot it," said Cole. "Put it down so it ain't got to suffer all day no more."

I locked eyes with the puling thing and realized I agreed.

But when I was sixteen, I happened upon Miss Tois in a grocery aisle. She was polite, asked about my parents, commented on my growth and how pretty I'd become, that she still couldn't help but see the little girl who used to wander around her house every summer.

I asked her about the dog.

"Who, Luther?" she asked. "Oh he's still with us. Sad old thing is too stubborn to die."

5

THE FISHY, ANIMAL SMELL of shit wakes Leland, and in a matter of seconds, he's uncovered the secret guest in Thad's room. It's still dark outside. Leland hasn't let himself realize I put it there even when I'm prying the phone from his hand. He thinks he's protecting me, keeps warning me not to open Thad's door, not comprehending my voice, "Put the phone down, put the phone down." So afraid of the moment, his mind won't let him walk backward yet: *how did this happen*?

I'm answering his hysteria with ambiguous nonsense.

"Don't go in Thad's room, Tessie, stay right here," he says.

"I know," I answer.

"Stay right here beside me," he says.

"I *know*, Leland," I answer.

He doesn't want to tell me what he saw, believes the image will shatter me. But I have already shattered, and he doesn't see me, and it isn't fair that, like a heavy vase, he hit the ground without shattering. So, to break him, I grip his arm and look up at him with madness in my eyes.

"I put it there," I say, pulling at him, but he can't hear me, just says, "Tessie, stop it," like I don't understand that he needs to make some important calls. So I say it again, "I put the alligator in Thad's room," and the sound of our son's name on my lips jars him. Then he's charging up and down the halls, going on about how he "can't do this, Tessie," and diving in and out of medicine cabinets, shaking empty prescription bottles in my face, asking, "How many were in here, Tessie?" Saying to himself, "And I just turn a blind eye, don't I?"

I have to chase him, to put my hands on his face so that he'll hear me, and I ask, "Did you see it, Leland? It's the one. It's the same one from that day."

. . .

When I started to show, people would ask me about pregnancy like it was a concept I had invented or that I oversaw. Isn't it incredible? Isn't it strange? To have a human being growing inside you! I would smile in the tradition of polite Southern conversation, not wanting to offend with honesty. It did not, to me, seem strange or incredible. It felt familiar. It felt important. I was participating in something ancient. Something cosmic and divine.

I slept on my side and cradled my growing stomach. He was so close, my baby. He the egg, my body the nest. Leland talked to my belly, made jokes about my waddling gait and shifting shape, but he was a supporter and a spectator—I alone could do this for our son. An alligator's incubation period, I would later learn, is about 65 days, but it takes more than four times as long to incubate a person. The animal kingdom is replete with threat, and all burgeoning life struggles against the crushing jaws of a world that wants to eat it. Newly hatched sea turtles can barely close the distance of a beach without being devoured, the ocean a mocking haven of nearness as one by one, babies are seized by the beaks of plunging birds. Of those to reach the sea, many are torn apart by the serrated teeth of reef sharks. Others avoid the mouths of predators only to become entangled in garbage.

Unable to escape, a grave of trash.

The civilized efficiency of human pregnancy and delivery are not safe from encroaching death. The fertilized egg might implant outside of the uterus and become doomed. The placenta might cover the entire opening of the uterus. The baby's heart might fail to accomplish the standard 120 to 160 beats per minute and be declared arrhythmic. The baby might rush prematurely from the safety of the womb and be confined to an incubator, deprived of its mother's arms, the new world a menace of unloving machines. The baby might swim itself upright in the womb or strangle itself with the cord meant to keep it alive, or become stuck, suffocated, broken, violating the contract of arrival.

These things I considered in the summer of 1987.

I mentioned them, nonplussed, to Leland, who immediately dismissed these concerns as inappropriate, saying, "Think about what will go right, not what could go wrong." But Leland didn't understand that I was neither pessimistic nor afraid. I had become powerful, a monolith of solidity. Primal in my maternal imperative, I was a wolf mother in the inhospitable wilderness of life, bearing my fangs at any darkness poised to swallow up my cub in death.

Do not fuck with me. I am calm but serious.

This duty ran through the network of my veins like blood—and I loved it. I was not afraid. I was in love.

My labor was punctual. The contractions set in, and Leland was the good man I knew him to be. He cared for me, helped me. In a wheelchair, my forehead beading with sweat, I surveyed the now-familiar hospital surroundings and thought about an argument I'd had in seminary. One of my classmates was celebrating his understanding of Genesis 2 and his admirable appreciation of women. "The Word calls woman a 'helper' to man. I'm grateful to the Lord that my wife is my helper."

I scoffed. "Yeah, but isn't the Hebrew word *ezer*? That word shows up all over the place to describe God, right? So whatever it means, it isn't that you're the boss. Unless you're God's boss as well."

That word, *ezer*, "one who helps," sounded romantic in the hospital waiting room. Leland as ezer to me. Me as ezer to our baby. God as ezer to all of us. I was in love.

In the delivery room, a calm resolve overtook me, empowered me. I was suffused with purpose. I did not bow to the painful work of laboring, nor to the uncomfortable insertion of an amniotic hook to break my water when my body refused to do so of its own volition. Leland admired me then. I could see it. He could see my resolve, that I had prepared for this, that I was neither frail nor fretful. I was the mother wolf in the snow.

And Leland wept when he saw Thad. It was like a battlefield silenced, the delivery room, my nakedness and bleeding so far from my mind that I was taken elsewhere, a euphoric trance.

My mother kept a framed painting in the kitchen of my childhood home. It was a white sanded beach, the sea beyond it a serene turquoise. I asked about this painting only once, and my mother told me that her father painted it in a place called Da Nang while at war. The painting, I thought, seemed to depict no war at all. My grandfather had included three small human figures on the beach.

"Who are they?" I asked.

"He didn't say," my mother answered absently,

wiping the table with an old rag though the table was perfectly clean.

I thought of my grandfather's painting in the delivery room, and for a moment, I was there. Leland, me, and our baby. The turquoise sea calm, the war over.

The spell broke when Leland reminded me, we'd yet to arrive at a name.

"Thad," I said, my voice choked with tears.

Leland smiled, moving sweat-drenched strings of hair from my forehead.

"Your granddaddy's name," he said. "Thad it is."

The mother wolf settled in the snow, gathering her cub to the safety of her side. For once, the forest was still.

. . .

Leland is touching the wound on his face, drawing his hand back to examine the blood on his fingers, then doing it again as if the first test could be faulty.

"Tessie," he says, perplexed. "Tessie, this isn't right."

When he attempted to carry me from the house, I struggled hopelessly and, in flailing desperation, raked two fingernails down his cheek. We are both shocked. I feel defensive. "You were hurting me," I say, though this isn't really true, and the pain I see in his face makes me regret saying it. I try to revise my statement. "You weren't listening," I say. "I want to stay here."

"Tessie," he keeps saying, like he's trying to steady an animal, to calm a growling dog. I'm sickened by the sound of my own name.

"We're just going to drive to get my dad so he can help me move it. He's done this before."

I know then that Leland doesn't see what I see, or that he won't.

"I'll wait outside," I say, making a show of my deep breathing, that I'm coming to my senses now, in my right mind.

"I want you to come with me."

"I just want to sit outside and calm down, Leland," I tell him, sanity restored to my voice. He doesn't answer, but I can see in his face that he has surrendered.

Leland walks me to the front porch where he watches me sit, like a suspicious parent, before he climbs silently into his truck. Even from a distance, I can see the red streaks on his face as he drives away.

Thad's room seems different by day. There's mustiness in the air and the immediate assault of swampy animal stench. Things are more disordered than I remembered. Ruben is less placid. He snaps at the air as I open the door, a deep, resonant hiss issuing from his open mouth. Was his tongue always that pale pink color? Almost white? I move quickly, sidling along the wall to get behind him, but when I lean to seize his tail, Ruben whirls around and bites my arm.

The strength of the bite, the brutality of it, is unbelievable. Ruben pulls me to the carpet with a single jerk. It feels like several grown men are wrenching my arm. I don't scream or cry, just sort of grunt and wheeze. Ruben releases me.

There is now an irregular zigzag of puncture marks running down my forearm, each of which immediately boils over, thick rivulets of blood snaking over my purpled flesh.

My work is not thwarted, only stalled. I reach for the tail again, this time stepping backward, out of bite range, and manage to grab hold of it. Ruben seems resigned to my handling him, and in a panting surge of adrenaline, I begin to haul him backward out of the room, my arm bleeding on the carpet as we go.

When I stop to open the French doors, Ruben crawls back into the living room, and I scream and dive for his tail, toppling over in the process and landing on him instead. He bends sideways, hissing, bites my leg twice, and lets go. It hurts less than my throbbing arm, but in an instant, the blood appears, and the pain seems to pool in my foot, which feels as if it might erupt. I stagger to my feet and start over. The alligator soils the carpet. I step in it, sliding, nearly compromising my footing. Feral desperation overtakes me. I grab his tail and haul Ruben into the yard, every muscle in my body screaming, threatening to snap.

I close the distance between the French doors and the work shed without incident. Thanks to Leland's organized cleanliness, Ruben has the openness of the shed to himself, surrounded by tool chests and mounted gardening implements. Once he's inside, I release Ruben's tail and hobble past him, slamming the door behind me.

My arm and leg are a crimson sheen of blood. I stumble, nauseous, making my way back to the front porch. I am smeared in blood and shit, my legs quivering in the cold when Leland and his father pull into the driveway.

• • •

Here is something I regret: after marrying Leland, I hardly spoke to my sister. Peyton had distanced herself from the strange circus of my seminary venture, had made no effort to visit me in Atlanta, didn't call. I knew that she was intimidated by me, expected me to be the one to close the gap, so when I returned home, I insisted my presence upon her. I took her to movies or to miniature golf, asked her pointed questions, became emotionally confrontational. I was a discolored link in the successive chain of my family hierarchy, an enigma, but Peyton was further down the chain than me. I outranked her. A small part of Peyton kept the mysterious wonder of her older sister locked away in the darkness of her heart and wanted to be like me, to know me, to supplant me. It rose from the top of her head like a wisp of emerald steam, this wonder, and I used it to organize her into the emptied reservoirs of need in my own life. She walled herself off, feigned resentment, but came as I beckoned, an ant in service to the queen.

When I married Leland, the once endlessly open shelves of my psyche became occupied. Happily so. There was no longer any need to conduct Peyton, but since I had done so for years, she waited for me to stir. I knew this but justified my sisterly hibernation on the basis of any of her previous transgressions against me. I pursued her, I thought, now she can pursue me. Of course, I had not established the exchange to work this way, so I knew she would not come but would instead wait on me and despair. I was last in my family to know when she got sick.

Illness, in the South, is undignified. A private matter. Not polite. I didn't realize that what Peyton had was schizophrenia until, at the squirming chagrin of my parents, I followed a nurse into the hospital hallway and asked for a clear diagnosis. My parents were, from the outset, encoding this horrible turn of events with inoffensive catchphrases. "Peyton is not doing too good right now, but we're praying for her," they told me in the beginning.

They took to sanitizing the word "schizophrenia" by

calling it "the problem" or "a hard time."

"Your sister's having a hard time right now."

Somewhere down the dark corridors of madness and the drugs sent in to make it behave, my sister must have been trapped. I couldn't find her. One Sunday afternoon, I'd had lunch at my parent's house, and she was there. Eyeing me with postured indifference but radiating loneliness. When next we spoke, the girl I knew had been replaced by a new one.

My dad had the unsurprising gall to theologize the horror of it all with a laughable patchwork of nonsense. He tightened his arthritic grip on my shoulder and said things like, "Tess, the Lord giveth and the Lord taketh away." The ridiculousness of these platitudes bothered me less than the nerve of him saying "giveth" and "taketh" without irony.

For a while, I hovered nervously around the impenetrable black box of my sister's fate as if there were some way to resolve its seamlessness. I called, visited, asked questions, researched treatments. The frustration set in, and with it, the effort to survive. Starving and cold, I began to gnaw at my trapped leg.

What can *I* do, really? Is this healthy for *me*?

The leg came free, eventually.

Today my parents talk about Peyton—who has been exiled to the second story of their home and fed a steady supply of antipsychotics—as if she were an unsightly skin disease to be treated with ointments. People will visit, arrange their faces in masks of sugary pity and ask, "And how is Miss Peyton doing?" My parents become mirrors of their ridiculous expressions and say things like, "She's doing real good. Real good. Just keep her in your prayers." And the exchange, a ritual of pleasantries, will conclude with the agreement: "We sure will. We sure will." But pray for what, exactly? No one has said, nor will anyone actually pray. My parents conduct this parody of concern with more seriousness than they do Peyton's treatment.

When Thad was taken from me, I became the new focus of this dance. "And how is Tessie doing?" "Keep her in your prayers." "We sure will." Like Peyton, I was snatched from decency by something horrible. We don't realize how vulnerable we are. Something with teeth is waiting for everyone.

• • •

It made the most sense to lie about what had happened. The door to Thad's room, I claim, was somehow left ajar, and "the animal" had crawled out. I panicked, attempted to move it, and was attacked. I collapse into Leland's arms, a rational damsel, traumatized, and he receives me with only a thin edge of skepticism.

My father-in-law, already terrified of women, maintains a safe distance unless summoned. I had always known I was expected to address my father-in-law as a Mr. Last Name, but I could never bring myself to say it, so I just called him Randy, and if it bothered him, he never said so. For his part, I couldn't remember Randy ever saying my name either, calling me only Tiny Girl, which I couldn't help but find endearing. Leland had no sisters, and Randy seemed to understand me as some kind of mysterious proxy daughter. My name, I think, felt too intimate, overreaching. When Randy registers my awful state—the blood and wild eyes—he looks like someone who has happened upon an impending suicide, driven by instinct to act but crippled by self-doubt, left to stand at a distance, hands raised as if this might be enough to stop something terrible from happening.

Together, the men search the outdoors surrounding our house, going as far as to wander beyond the toolshed, likely as a demonstration of meticulousness to set my mind at ease. Leland shakes the doors of the shed, ensures the lock, but does not enter. I remain calm.

It's probably Leland's concern for appearances that keeps me from the hospital. I tell him my injuries are treatable at home, that they aren't as bad as they look. I ask him to help me clean them, and without waiting, I enter the bathroom, pull the slip over my head, and climb into the tub. When Leland finally looks at me, I realize I have relinquished any claim to his lust. When he sees me, knees drawn up, nearly emaciated and smeared with blood, my limbs discolored and swelling, I can see heartbreak on his face and, behind it, revulsion. I am all bone and angles. I feel powerful in this moment.

Good, I think. If I can't inflame your desire, then I will aggravate your disgust.

Leland fills his cupped hands with warm water and pours it over my wounds, dabbing them clean with a white rag. With each gentle contact, the anger weeps from my wounds, and Leland wipes it away. The bloodied water pools beneath me and circles the drain, Leland swabbing my arm and leg, me wincing, tears in my eyes. He draws the rag back with each of my gasps, noticing my tears and saying, "I'm sorry," thinking it's physical pain that summons them. He doesn't (or cannot) realize what is really making me cry.

• • •

Why did I choose seminary to spite my father? Weren't there other, less invested ways to do this? When I was a little girl, my parents would decree that my dinner be eaten. What injustice is this, I thought, that I should be forced to consume that which I did not desire nor request? So I would refuse. My dad would extend his form over my plate and, touching the uneaten food, declare, "Now Tess, yer not gettin' up from this table until yah eat every last bite of that goddamn supper." My mother would grimace at the cruelty of the decree or at the swearing in it, but she would keep quiet, shaking her head.

This happened several times, I remember. I felt

something warm consolidate in my bones. The power of will. Why should I be made to do this, I would wonder, and then on the heels of the question an empowering realization:

I cannot be made to do this.

The untouchable resolve of my agency was a wall no one could climb, not even the southern expectation of dignified obedience. Let them force-feed me, I thought. Let them shovel the collard greens into my mouth, pried open by their violent hands. They can go that far, but it won't be me eating it. I am unassailable, I thought. I am the impasse.

This game would continue into the dark, me occupying an empty table, head lolling on the spongy spine of weariness. Peyton would sneak in, panicked by conflict, desperate for peace, and offer to eat the offending remains, but I wouldn't let her. "I want him to see it," I'd tell her, though she couldn't understand why. I would leer at her, my eyes cracked with veins. "I want him to find me in the morning and see that I didn't eat a single bite."

Isn't all of this—the game of agency—a challenge we lobby at God? Saint Augustine would argue it was

God's will that kept me at the table. John Wesley would say it was mine. All we can do is test the strings to see if they snap and set us free. Some of my life has felt like an effort to sharpen the scissors. The day that Thad was born, I felt my frustrated preoccupation with these strings dissolve. The corridor of my soul seemed to narrow, and rather than panic, I was relieved.

• • •

Bandaged and shivering, Leland wraps me in a towel and asks what I would like to wear. I feel elderly, infirmed. I ask for my pink slip and he tells me he "put it away," like it was an artifact that might scare me. He brings me one of his flannel shirts, something I wore to bed when we were dating, and my mind fusses over the gesture. Is there love in it? Pity? Both? He eases me into bed, pulling the blankets to my chin as if I were a child, and lies down beside me. I make a show of my grogginess, that I can barely keep my eyes open, then I wait in the dark for the tension in his body to release like a dull shockwave through the mattress.

With more at stake, I'm aware of every sound and

shifting shadow, and I tiptoe cartoon-like through the house to the groaning French doors, the work shed waiting in the wet haze of night.

I open the shed with calm resolve, not excited, driven by purpose. The backyard emanates a pale luster under the full moon, but the inside of the work shed is an inky well of black in the seconds before I flip the light switch. A low whine comes from somewhere in the dark. A delay, the brief crackle of stubborn electricity, and the ugly piss-colored light comes to life overhead. The solitary bulb creates as much shadow as it does light, but I see that Ruben has backed himself into the wall opposite the entrance and lies facing me, shuffling. In the shafts of shadow, I can see the alligator is overpowering some gleaming black shape. The scene is detached and otherworldly and for a moment I am outside of my body until I realize that Luther, our dog, is in the alligator's mouth. Luther struggles, whimpering, his front legs swimming in the air helplessly, slowing down, and Ruben flings the dog back and forth like a ragdoll, his panicked yelping transformed in an instant to a low, belabored wheeze. Luther's blood makes its way to my feet in slow, snaking trails. Ruben continues to bite, shake, and swallow. While the alligator is still gulping the torn carcass, it talks.

"Are you ready to go?"

"Where are we going?" I ask.

"You know where we have to go."

"I'm not ready."

He moves his head side to side, shifting his bulk with his front legs, snaps, and swallows more of the dog. He speaks again. "Very truly I tell you, when you were younger you dressed yourself and went where you wanted, but when you are old, you will stretch out your hands and someone else will dress you and lead you where you do not want to go."

"Not there," I say. "Not yet."

Ruben seems to look elsewhere. "We can go somewhere else."

Then we are in an old house. It is very cold. My breath becomes a white vapor before me. There is a shape in the darkness several feet away. "What is that?" I ask.

"A boy," says Ruben.

Then I see him. A small boy, maybe three or four years old, naked and shivering, bound to the baluster at the foot of a staircase. His mouth has been gagged, but I can hear his muffled, terrified sobs. I lurch forward, drawn by maternal instinct—*human* instinct—to the boy. Ruben stops me.

"We're not here. Not really."

And I see then the familiarity of it, this scene. My memory had painted it many times before.

"Is that Billy Gaffney?" I ask, knowing that Ruben will answer yes, and he does, so I say, "This is how I pictured it," thinking of the awful book I read about Albert Fish, the murderer of small children. Fish claimed to have left Billy Gaffney nude, bound in that abandoned house through a New York winter's night. Twelve hours would pass before Fish would return to torture him. I start crying. I draw both hands up to my heart, threading my fingers together, and take deep breaths to keep from fainting. "Why here?" I ask.

"Isn't this where you go?" Ruben asks, his eyes on the whimpering boy, whose little voice is hoarse from crying. "In your mind? To the place of most pain?"

"We shouldn't be here."

"The worst is yet to come."

"Please…"

"Bad place, the world," Ruben muses. "So much pain. This room, another room, everywhere."

I've closed my eyes. I'm listening to the blood thrum through my head, wanting to shut out the helpless tears in the distance. There's a sound outside, and I look to see daylight and a man that I know is Albert Fish carrying a small bag and approaching the house. "Please," I try to say again, but it comes out as air, white steam.

"You want to go to the other place?" Ruben asks.

I cover my mouth to keep from crying out, my eyes closed, and I shake my head, no. If it's between this place and that place, I can't. I try then to push from my mind what I know is coming, what I'd read several times. I look to see the boy, and for a horrible moment, our eyes lock and he seems with his to plead for help. But then the air around me warms, and I open my eyes, my heart pounding, to see we have returned to the work shed.

"Bad place," Ruben says again. "Here, there, all the same. Pain everywhere."

• • •

IN MAY OF 1980, a boy I didn't know presented me with a pornographic magazine. I was sitting in Savannah High School's auditorium, the creaking wooden theater chair cutting into my back. Friends of mine, girls, on either side, we were laughing about something, the end of the school year encroaching, everything nebulous.

I heard my name, hissed, like air from a tire, all consonants. Behind me, a cluster of boys, awkward and sweating in the stale, musty air, became one collective and debauched grin. One of them—the one hissing my name—handed over a worn roll of glossy paper, half of the book folded backward to reveal a full-page spread within. The headline read, "Southern Belles." In the middle of a painfully phony-looking bayou-themed set sat a nude woman, her legs spread wide for a gaudy reveal of her vulva. She'd positioned her arms like rigid columns on either side of her torso, pressing her already significant breasts together, torpedo-like, for exaggerated lift. Beneath her, a taxidermy alligator acted as a perch for her ridiculous pose. It was the first time I'd seen something so unapologetically lewd. I remember a distinct pang of curiosity and discomfort overlapping, like beholding a corpse.

"Looks just like you," the boy said to the audible approval of his sniggering comrades.

I looked again. He was right; the naked woman seemed to somehow mirror me, a vulgar doppelganger. I saw then my own visage staring back at me, my own brazen figure and bared genitals, and I was seized by desperation to cover my nakedness. I tore the page from the magazine, wadding it into a crumpled ball and threw it at the boy.

"Fucking bitch," he snarled. He reached out and grabbed a shock of my hair, wrenching my head backward with an vicious tug.

When he'd released me, I leaned forward, elbows on my knees, pinning the magazine, my eyes welling with tears. A dull throb coiled around my vertebrae, wounding down the curve of my aching neck. Each of my female companions fell silent with shock.

After the assembly, I disappeared into the sluggish crowd of socializing teenagers, moving wordlessly to the women's restroom where I disposed of both the magazine and, after taking one final look, my amputated doppelganger. In the hall beyond the bathroom, I overheard a group of onlookers debriefing the incident.

"Oh, you know she just loved the attention," one girl said.

"Did you notice she didn't even disagree?" another girl asks. "He was like, 'Tessie, this stacked bombshell looks like you,' and she basically said, 'Sure does!'"

"I can actually understand being pissed if someone just ripped up something that belonged to me," the first girl said.

When I could tell the group had moved on, I left the bathroom and caught up with them as if I'd been looking for them all along.

"Oh my gosh, Tessie, are you okay?" one of them asked.

"Yeah," I said, rubbing my neck.

"Those guys were being so gross," the other girl said.

"I know," I agreed. "That picture didn't even look like me."

Physical intimacy, in high school, seemed to me like an amateur playing drums. Something in nearly every person, when they see drums, wants to be given permission to hit them without restraint, though few of us know how to do it with any real rhyme or reason. If we are allowed to hit them, we are, in that moment, satisfied by release and disappointed by our ineptitude. We know even then that if we could do it right, we would be more satisfied still.

I fumbled through a few crude sexual encounters before Leland, like a starving person who eats to survive but not to enjoy. The stories that the boys told never quite matched what had actually happened.

With Leland, I saw in our rhythmic and sweating passion a kind of expertise, two beings fastening themselves together, one flesh. All of us, I guessed, want to be joined to someone else, to ask the cosmic question of loneliness and answer it with panting confidence: no, someone knows me, and I know them back. But in the compulsory, hormonal pairing devoid of love, we make one another objects for consumption, like predatory beings, each thing devouring the other with no purpose but the feeding.

On the walk home from school, I remember sweat running down my lower back. I was clutching my schoolbooks to my chest, wanting to cover myself, the dirty magazine mimic making me self-conscious about my body. Taking a detour down winding dirt roads to avoid the foot traffic of other dispersing students, I happened upon a little boy, shirtless, squatting at the edge of an unkempt yard, pulling the twitching legs from a giant grasshopper.

"Hey!" I barked, suddenly furious. "Put that down!"

The boy looked up, horrified, releasing the grasshopper to drop in soft dirt and turn itself in a pathetic little circle without really going anywhere.

Stupid words came out of my mouth. "You shouldn't do that."

The boy squinted up at me, bewildered at the crying teenage girl that had suddenly materialized in the summer heat to scold him.

"I ain't killt it," the boy said.

Beyond the yard was a shitty ramshackle house with open windows out of which came the screaming of a man and a woman. All my attention went there, scared, forgetting the boy and the grasshopper. The screen door blew open, and a bearded man in a torn, sagging t-shirt and no pants came shoving a crying woman, seizing her by her ponytail.

The little boy turned from the scene, embarrassed, and set to work drawing shapes in the dirt with his long blackened fingernail, pretending to be consumed by this new work of his, oblivious to the world.

The woman was flailing, kicking, struggling against the man before he sent her to the ground with a powerful shove. The skirt of her faded summer dress flipped as she tumbled, revealing bruised legs and no underwear. I shuffled backward, frozen with panic and fear as the man, his face glistening with sweat, reared up a knobby arm and brought his bony knuckles down into the woman's face with several wet, rapping jabs. The woman's shrieking was broken only by the blows, like a skipping record, then becoming a low gurgling whimper.

"Fucking bitch," the man said. He spit in the grass, panting.

At my feet, I saw that the boy had drawn a ring in the dirt around the injured grasshopper, an unremarkable barrier mocking the insect's suffering. If the grasshopper could somehow cross the line, maybe it could escape this awful thing happening to it. But if it could cross the line at all, this awful thing wouldn't be happening in the first place.

4

I PLAY A TERRIBLE game of lasts. I think of the last meal Thad ever ate, the last time he saw stars, the last time he walked in the warm water of the Georgia coast.

It was June. Thad insisted on wearing his blue goggles though he would never learn to immerse his head in the water, never learn to swim, never visit the beach again. With inflated water wings on either arm and the silly-looking goggles on his forehead like a scuba diver, Thad ran, my hand in his, through the foamy surf, laughing, elated. At home, in the bath, splashing was against the rules, but here he could splash me, and I could splash him, and neither the sand nor the watery horizon seemed to end at all.

Leland and I buried him in the sand. He could barely contain his joy, wanting so badly to erupt from the warm bonds, but we made him wait.

"Not yet," we teased. "Just a little more sand." And

he would laugh, practically shaking, drunk on his own joy.

When he emerged, the sand cracked like an old casing, and he rose up before me, his little arms lifted over his skinny frame, silhouetted by the sun, this boy that grew in my womb, that I held and nursed and sang to sleep, now a standing, speaking person.

Even if I knew then it was the last time we'd ever visit the beach as a family, I would have done everything exactly the same way.

• • •

In the morning, Leland calls my office and tells them I won't be showing up for work. I can tell he wants to obscure his secrecy—the sneaking to the living room, calling without asking me, almost whispering into the receiver. I want to move to the door and hear what he's saying, but when I attempt standing, my veins pump molten lava into my leg and arm, and it's everything I have not to collapse.

Dragging myself across the carpet toward the door, I can hear him talking to someone, presumably my boss

Jerry, mentioning in a serious voice what he calls a "bit of a wild day over here," some mumbling, then some dismissive "Oh, she's fine, she's fine" and then, in an even more controlled whisper, "It's the damnedest thing, Jerry, after what we've been through, but you know we're taking it one day at a time and I hope Tess and I will be able to laugh about this later."

My bandages are now dotted with burgundy. I drag myself into our bathroom and haul myself up on the counter. Every one of my prescription bottles is empty, but I don't remember how they got that way. Wasn't there a moment yesterday, Leland shaking them at me? Were they empty then, or did he empty them? My pink slip is in the sink, soaking. It looks like a prop from a horror movie. I set to work replacing my bandages, dabbing the bite marks with peroxide, using a shaking index finger to fill the puckering red craters with ointment. Leland discovers me in my work and scolds me, gently urges my hand away from the wounds. He's like a nurse calming a dementia patient that somehow got hold of a butcher knife. "Let me, Tess," he says to dull the blade of insult like it's because he loves me, not because I exhaust him.

When he's completed his fussy doctoring, he invites me to lie down even though I am not tired, nor do I want to lie in bed all day.

"I called Jerry," he says.

"I know. I could hear you."

He looks flustered, recovers. "They'll be fine without you today. I think you should just get some rest."

"They'd be fine without me any day, Leland. I answer the phone. I file paperwork. I don't need to rest. I've got alligator bites, not the flu."

He winces. "I know what you have, Tessie. I just meant it might be good to take it easy for a day. It won't kill you to take it easy."

I look away from him, jut my chin. I am too far down the tunnel of indecency to salvage my credibility with Leland. Good Southern women do not fall apart. He resents me for this, I know. Leland has always been a man of order, of ideals. I love him for it, but his ideals have become a cleansing flood that purges me from the ordered respectability of his life. There was a wild, romantic intimacy in those early times, a clumsy entanglement of sex and adoration and congruence. But the more we hardened in the strangeness of who we are, the more rigid our edges, the greater the difficulty to fit the pieces together day after day. Soon, strange things started hurting.

I was hurt by the way Leland admired things. He would regale me about his great admiration for some asinine nugget of spiritual wisdom passed down by his father while the two of them cut grass—the way his father "knew" God. Had he admired me, his lunatic bride, who spent years and her grandmother's fortune to earn some useless sheet of paper to "know" God? Leland would describe a tree or a truck as beautiful, but not me. Not anymore. He handed out kindness and praise to people he knew half as well. If it was insincere, it was worse. He couldn't even bring himself to fake it with me.

Leland, I knew, believed I was wallowing. Everyone else, he thought, pulled themselves together and endured while I was coming apart. Hadn't he suffered too? Hadn't he lost so much? But his face was a hardened mask of resolve that disguised his hurting if he was hurting at all. What he thought I wanted from this, I wasn't sure. Was I feeling sorry for myself? Did I even want something from someone? I didn't have the answers to these questions.

Leland was erasing Thad.

"Why don't you call Ouida?" Leland asks without looking at me. "I know she would keep you company."

"While I just sit in bed?"

He throws his hands up and shakes his head. "It was just a suggestion, Tessie. You're obviously going to do whatever it is that you want to do."

None of this is what I want to do.

. . .

In the second chapter of Genesis, Moses details the creation of mankind by God. Skeptical readers love to pick on its supposedly embarrassing scientific inaccuracies, the goofy-sounding prose that ardent fundamentalists take too literally, unwilling to let it just say what it wants to say on its own terms. Both kinds of people seem to conveniently overlook that Genesis was written thousands of years ago in a very different time and place, informed by a very different way of seeing and understanding the world. The more I read it, the more I could see it. Like staring at a painting until it can't help but give up its secrets. In Genesis chapter two, Moses describes men and women as different but complementary components of a masterpiece. In this strange, ancient block of poetic prose, Moses admits to the way of things: men and women grow up and leave their parents, they get married, they become *one flesh.* In Hebrew, the pairing of "one" and "flesh" implies fusion at the deepest, most intimate level.

Sex with Leland was often that way.

We seemed hungry—desperate, even—to somehow bring ourselves into a holy and congruent union, the wet friction of his stomach against mine, his hipbones hammering against me, his strong hands gripping my waist from behind. The way he would thread his fingers through my hair, fasten his hands around my shoulder, the way I would close my legs around him, all of it the fevered work of becoming one flesh. We were more than mating animals then, more than upright apes satisfying a biological appetite. We were man and wife, one flesh, a cosmic union, caught up in a story as old as the universe.

In seminary, my classmates liked to embarrass me with the Bible's explicit sexuality. Laughing, eyeing me across the room during lectures that unpacked the elaborate erotic metaphors in The Song of Solomon. One boy asked the professor, deliberate and contrived, "Since Eve was made from Adam, is that why she's incomplete unless she becomes one flesh with him?"

"She's not incomplete," the professor said, bored and diplomatic. "Becoming one flesh is not about the incomplete being made whole. It's about two unique and whole people coming together to form a new and unique union."

Lately, I feel like a woman torn apart.

• • •

I stumble out of the bedroom when I'm convinced I've given Leland enough time to leave for work. Seized by panic, I actually gasp at the state of the house. Beyond closing Thad's bedroom door, Leland hasn't done anything to restore order, which is worrying. He's either given up, or he wanted me to see what he saw. There are spirals of mud and alligator droppings hardened in the carpet. One of the couch cushions is torn. Dark speckles of my blood are everywhere. I find another empty prescription bottle on the floor beside two library books I don't remember borrowing, one of which has dozens of random words like "house," "barren," and "killed" removed by a hobby knife I find nearby. There's a drop of dried blood on the hobby knife.

There are several Styrofoam trays in the sink that were, presumably, recently the beds of various refrigerated meats. A can of SpaghettiOs sits opened on the corner, but its contents are undisturbed. It occurs to me now that Leland's suggestion to summon Ouida was likely passive-aggressive or in the vain hope that, applying his suggestion, Ouida would see all this and be stirred to some action Leland doesn't think he can accomplish himself.

I feel strangely buoyant. It doesn't take long for a handful of ibuprofen to dull the throbbing in my arm and leg, and the seepage from my wounds is minimal while I clean. The mud and alligator shit lift with relative ease, but the blood only spreads. I call the first three carpet cleaners listed in the yellow pages, frustrated with their unwillingness to come right away, and surprise myself by asking the third number why "every goddamn carpet cleaner in Savannah is so fucking busy they can't clean the blood out of my carpet today."

The first crying fit happens when I attempt to discard the can of SpaghettiOs. I knew when I saw it, of course, that the can was Thad's, but I gun the realization down in cold blood and move on. When I *touch* the can, however, the realization, not dead after all, stirs. It bolts upright and grabs me by the wrist, wanting to pull me down, to pull me into itself, the memory a pool of black quicksand. My legs shake, suddenly boneless, and I crumple, my face colliding with the countertop on the way down. I don't realize until I'm on the ground that I'm gripping the can. I open my hand over the jagged lid, pried open like a mouth, and close my fist around it until I feel the metal bite through my flesh, and the pain outside is enough to distract, if only for a moment, from the pain inside. I can breathe again—it comes like the first gulp of air from someone nearly drowned.

I move on from the incident, shuddering with each inhalation, steadying myself on quivering legs, and wrap a flowery paper towel around the gash in my palm that yawns open every time I open and close my fingers. I get dressed, put on makeup again.

This is good, I think. I'm taking control of the day.

I'm applying lipstick with a hand that feels like it's on fire when I hear someone shuffling around on the front step. My immediate suspicion is that it's Ouida, that she'll let herself in, see the state of the house and fly into a frenzy. I feel an intense surge of anger toward Leland. While I prepare answers to the questions I suspect Ouida will ask, I eventually deduce that whoever is making noise outside isn't coming in.

I move cautiously to the front door, attempting to peer through a frosted glass pane in its center, and I see the shape of someone who, as a blurry silhouette, seems theatrically distressed, like a panicked mime. He paces the doorstep—a five-foot lap—leans over, stands up, grabs his face, kneels, runs his hands over his head, starts the whole ordeal over again. I realize watching this blurred shape that maybe I should be wary of this spectacle, but it seems too strange to trouble me. The shape leans a final time, then turns to flee the porch. I hear a car driving away. When I open the door, there's a VHS tape on the doormat.

Fixed to it, a note that reads, "I tried to destroy it but couldn't. Really bad dreams. Please forgive me. Only trying to do what's right. I can't be the one to do it. God bless."

. . .

When Thad was a baby, I became an expert in ignoring the great cavalcade of wisdom from older, and therefore, wiser mothers to go before me. All of them convinced that their methods of nursing, rocking, burping, changing diapers, naps, all of them had been tested and were therefore superior to whatever young, naïve, and foolhardy methods I'd employed. However unique, arbitrary, or contradictory these motherly techniques, they had been used by women with more experience, so I was expected to bow before their experiential expertise, grateful, and apply it without question.

Other moms, even moms whose babies arrived mere weeks before mine, treated me as if I had climbed into an airplane and was insisting on flying it without bothering to consult them, the very ones who designed the airplane and built it from the ground up. Southern women observed Thad's every whimper or squirm, diagnosed it in an instant, then said, "You know, what you ought to do is..."

Knowing me, Leland assumed I would respond by rejecting these nuggets of wisdom with bold confidence, but I mostly nodded and accepted some while only pretending to apply others. These women didn't bother me because they didn't know Thad. I couldn't imagine feeling anxious about the way someone else understood my mothering. I was his mother. Only me.

I never assumed Thad was so darling, so unique in all the world, that he was beyond the advice of others, that he should be raised in a bubble of his own preciousness, that all other children and mothers were hopeless before his undeniable specialness. Thad was a baby boy, in many ways like many other baby boys, but he was mine, and I loved him. Like both Leland's and mine, Thad's hair grew a soft, shimmering blonde in his first two years before it darkened, a chestnut brown, and hung in a wild, messy mop around his cherub face. I learned early on that some children squirm in their parent's embrace, restless, unwilling to be handled for long, but Thad fit comfortably into Leland's arms and mine and stayed there for hours. He smiled more than he didn't.

Leland was a good father. I didn't doubt he would be. Shaped by the affection he missed from his own dad, he lavished Thad with fatherly warmth, kissed his face regularly. Like a man arranging something to fit into an empty space, Leland made more and more room in his heart for his son. Southern men do not often love their sons well, but something in Leland's genetic coil was compelled to adore Thad, helpless against it. Southern men want protégés to supplant them, to shake their hands with respectful dignity, to send them to football fields, factories, and war. Leland was caught up in the messy whirlwind of love. Shameless, he spun Thad in the air, laughing, kissed his neck, watched him sleeping. My heart would swell at the sight of them, my soul flooded with a painful, staggering joy. Why, I wondered, had men stumbled over the thresholds of their own homes after work or travel or battle and found what was once familiar now alien and estranged? How do these cords of intimacy unravel? I wasn't afraid. I felt enveloped in love. The mother wolf could thaw the snow, her alpha watchful, a sentry in the night.

• • •

When Ouida lets herself in, I'm facedown in the living room carpet, clutching the VHS tape, groaning. She rushes to me, turns me over in a panic, seems bewildered and scared. I blink hard, forcing tears from my stinging eyes, and affect a clumsy air of calm.

"What's up?" is all I can think to say.

"*What's up*?" Ouida echoes. "What are you doing? What's going on?" She surveys the living room. "What happened in here?"

"Did Leland call you?" I sneer.

She seems oblivious. "What is that?" she asks, reaching for the tape.

"Thad."

Ouida sighs. "Get up, Tess. Let's clean this up."

I pull away from her, roll over into a fetal position clutching the tape. Ouida wanders off. A few seconds later, I can hear her yelling about SpaghettiOs being splattered everywhere and why is there blood on the linoleum. My eyes feel like they've been scoured with sandpaper. "I need a break," I'm yelling for some reason, but she doesn't hear me, she's grunting about the smell and the dirt. "I need a break, Ouida, tell Leland!"

She appears above me. "Get up, Tessie."

"Just a few days to myself. He doesn't understand, Ouida."

"*I* don't understand, Tessie. I don't understand why you have blood and dog shit all over your damn living room, and I'm about fed up with all this nervous breakdown shit. I mean it."

I sniff. "It's not dog shit," I say. I stand, wobbling, still holding the tape to my chest. "I'm not having a nervous breakdown."

"Whatever kind of episode this is supposed to be," Ouida says, her hands in front of her as if to indicate the world around us. "You have to get it together, Tessie." She scans me for signs of lucidity, seems to notice my bandages for the first time. "What happened to you? Jerry said you had an accident."

I feel dizzy. I realize through a haze of recognition that I might be shivering. "I am taking it one day at a time," I say, my voice sounding discernibly insane even to me. Ouida seems to shift from frustration to fear. She reaches out to steady me.

"I want you to come stay with me a night or two," she says.

"I can't. I just need to be alone, Ouida. Leland is not letting me. Tell him to just give me some space just for a day or two."

"I'm not sure this house can handle another day of you having space."

"This wasn't me, Ouida. Will you please talk to Leland?"

She stares at me, breathes deep, purses her lips. "Hand me that tape."

"I'm not watching it. It's just Thad at tee-ball. I just wanted to hold it."

Ouida touches me then, moves a lock of stringy hair from my forehead, then puts her hand on my face, the darkness of her skin contrasting my pallid, anemic cheek.

. . .

There is a park two blocks from our house that Thad loved, encircled by sprawling live oaks fanning their great branches out over the park benches where I would sit and watch him exhaust himself on the small playground. Tourists would come and go, snapping photographs of the dangling Spanish moss.

Near the children's play structure stood an upright xylophone fixed to a pole about three feet high. Long metal cylinders act as the instrument's keys, and a dangling, rubber-sheathed mallet is tethered to the apparatus by a nylon cord. Panting and dappled with sweat, children climb rope ladders, swing on the swing sets, descend the slide, then occasionally run over to this xylophone, clumsily grappling at the mallet and—with little focus or purpose—beat the iron cylinders with chaotic fury. The resulting dissonance—a wobbling metallic din—forever haunts the park, an eerie soundtrack to the clamoring children that I eventually learned to ignore.

Thad, like any other kid, was drawn to the xylophone but, finding no way to draw an actual song out of it, almost immediately tired of its insolubility, like a Rubik's Cube. One afternoon, I remember, he became uncharacteristically preoccupied with it. When it was time to walk home, I approached the xylophone and found him tapping each of its keys curiously, as if he were testing them.

"Are you playing a song, Thaddy?" I asked him.

"I can't do it, Mama," he said.

"What do you mean?"

He tapped a few keys in demonstration, the disharmony obvious.

"I think it sounds pretty," I said.

And Thad looked up at me then with express disappointment on his small face. The disappointment was not with the imperfection of his performance but with my lying about it.

He never played that xylophone again.

...

With Ouida gone, I load the tape into the bedroom VCR. My heart racing, nearly audible, blood pulsing like a painful strobe light in my skull, I wait through more than a minute of flickering static and white noise. I'm somehow both disappointed and relieved in equal measure, and I fast-forward the tape, prepared to find nothing when the image of a half-dozen children in matching green t-shirts appears on the screen. In a frenzy, I eject the tape and resume clutching it to my chest, hyperventilating, and I say, "It's there," over and over again, crying. The team was gathering by the lake for their picture, all of them squinting in the merciless Georgia sun. Before I stopped the tape, at that moment when the image populated the TV screen like a foul placard, I could see one little boy leaning over the water's edge, the way he always would, looking for animals.

The ringing phone wakes me up, and I rise from the bedroom floor, my face burning from the shag carpet that's left an ugly series of pink marks across my cheek.

Answering the phone seems important. "Hello?"

"Hey," comes Leland's voice. I don't say anything, not knowing how, until he speaks again. "Tessie?"

"What?"

He sighs. "I talked to Ouida."

"I know."

A silence lingers. "She said she wants you to come stay with her for a night, but that if you won't come, it might be good for you to have the house to yourself for the night."

"Okay."

"To have some space."

"Okay."

Leland sighs dramatically, again, then says, "I can stay at my dad's, but Tess…" There's a sound, breathing maybe. "I'm worried, Tess."

I think for a moment, annoyed and at a loss, and realize that Leland is crying. My chest tightens. This is a sound I've never heard. The floodgates of my compassion, my adoration for this man burst forth, and I'm immediately overcome with violent sobs that shudder my entire frame. Through my whimpering, I'm saying, "I love you," I'm saying, "I just need a break," I'm saying, "One day at a time." The mother wolf howling at the moon.

I think it's important to wait for night before I return to the shed. Things get bad while I wait. I have another crying fit because *Wings* isn't on, and I beat the remote control against the television until it cracks. *Wheel of Fortune* blares obnoxiously while I gather the spilled SpaghettiOs in my hands and eat them, unable to fathom simply throwing the mess away. I don't hear from Leland, so I assume he went straight from work to his father's house. I try to imagine how he might describe the predicament to other people, mortified that the veneer of our perseverance is eroding. To keep spectators at ease, Leland will sometimes balance the right amount of false transparency with a particular brand of pain-free resilience that bystanders come to expect from the grieving. He'd say, "Tess is just missing Thad tonight," the sound of our son's name on his lips an uncomfortable jolt, but surely this man who can speak so candidly is grieving well.

Dusk seems violet outside, edged with pink and smeared with grey clouds, an ominous night falls. The light flickers on in the shed. Ruben is there, motionless, a cloud of flies hovering over congealed cakes of my dog's blood.

...

Shortly after I'd begun my secret collection of newspaper clippings, I saw a young mother weeping into a camera on the morning news. It was a warm morning in July, piercing beams of sunlight cutting through our kitchen window, casting long white shafts across the white tiled surface of our island table. Standing statuesque before a burbling coffee machine, the weeping woman's words fired arrows through the fog of my misery, and I turned on my heels, leaning into the tiny TV, eclipsing it, pinching the volume knob and rocking it counterclockwise so Leland wouldn't hear and rush to my rescue. The world believes the grieving so frail that a slight breeze—the mere mention of death—can collapse us. But we have already been collapsed. We've been brought all the way down. We can't be *reminded* of death, it is ever before us, on our backs, a horrible crouching goblin that grows, fixed to our shoulders, sinking us.

I couldn't believe this woman was telling her story on television this way. Just days prior, her two-year-old son had been "helping" her load laundry into the washer. They'd used a footstool so he could drop his own tiny t-shirts into the soapy water. A few minutes later, she was wandering their home, mindlessly seeing to chores, when she noticed, passively, that she hadn't seen or heard her son in minutes. She called out to him and heard nothing. Her calm exploration became panicked pacing in and out of every room, her voice rising, crying out for him to cancel the horrible dread of something soon to ruin her. She went outside, screaming, then back to the awful laundry room. Dipping a single hand into the clouded suds, she felt him, tangled and submerged. She had to enlist a neighbor's help to retrieve his lifeless body from the machine.

And here was this woman on my TV, her eyes behind tiny glass windows of tears, her voice stilted, some mannered anchor patronizing her, "It's okay, it's okay." It was not okay. I hated her for dragging the awful creature of her grief out for the cameras, arranging it like a loathsome puppet, dancing it across the stage of every breakfast table in the tri-county area. I smashed the glass coffee carafe over the TV, a flying shard of broken glass opening my forearm like an envelope, my face was burned by the spray of boiling Folgers. The TV went on playing the news, the woman's voice uninterrupted. Leland rushed to the disturbance, found me wet and weeping, an embarrassing meltdown, and he cleaned in silence, afraid to stir the agitated horror of my insanity.

I thought about that woman for weeks. Like Billy

Gaffney, her drowned son became a lump of hot coal on my head, and I ran the scene in my mind on an incessant loop. I would close my eyes, taking shallow breaths, and imagine her swelling panic, the long shadow of encroaching dread extending before her, something with leathery black wings settling down on her back never to fly away.

Sitting in the darkness of my room, my heart hammering against my ribcage, I would draw a shaking hand out in the air before me and imagine I was her, about to dip my hand in that awful water, already knowing that which cannot be unknown, and I would find Thad there in the washer of my mind. I would imagine the washer growing, expanding until I could climb down into the water with him, cradle his cold body, a sodden doll. And then, at my fantasy's most extraordinary note of suffering, something surprising: I felt so relieved just to be holding him again.

. . .

Ruben's nose stirs the air as he lifts his head, exposing the soft white flesh of his throat. The cloud of flies disperses.

"Are you ready to go?" he asks.

"Let me go somewhere else," I say.

"There isn't much time."

"Just not yet. Somewhere else."

The hot wet air in the shed becomes suddenly dry. I inhale dust. My eyes adjust to the midday sun, and an image of sand-colored rock faces jutting from a rolling green hillside come into focus. I'm dizzied by the clamor of a noisy crowd and a human stink of sweat, blood, and shit. People are gathered before three large crosses where nude, shivering men hang, nailed up by their hands and feet. Others pass by the scene, unconcerned. Some or all of the hanged men, caked in browned blood, have soiled themselves. I turn at the sight of their shriveled penises, pubic hair matted with blood, and observe Ruben slithering in the gravelly dirt at the foot of the center cross. Looking again, cautiously, I can see the flesh of one of the hanging men is flayed, his face is blackened, a balloon of swelling like a purple crown of cauliflower. The men wheeze and quake on their crosses, an audibly wet, belabored breathing that makes me greedy for air.

"Why here?" I ask.

"Doesn't it matter to you?"

I look at the dying men again, some gibberish exchange of a throaty foreign language rumbling through the crowd. "Is this really it?"

"It's always like this."

I squint up into the faces of the hanging men. One of them begins to convulse, drooling. A few bystanders point and laugh.

"Undignified," Ruben says.

"Yes," I agree, not taking my eyes off of the crosses. "It doesn't seem…" I say, "noteworthy?" Some of the bystanders, bored, talk amongst themselves, others leave. "It's harder to look at than I thought it would be."

"Sheer volume of pain," Ruben says. "Hard to see how any of it matters."

I look to Ruben, rage heating the space behind my eyes. "But people remember this," I say through gritted teeth. "They care."

• • •

My mother made several attempts to console me during the four-day haze of my screaming, sobbing, collapsing, pounding my fists against things. She touched my swollen face, and with tearless condescension, she said, "Right now, it feels like your heart is breaking. But Tessie, you'll have other children, and you'll love them, and that crack in your heart will heal."

I was aghast then, snatching her hand away by the wrist. I glared into my mother's dumbfounded face, panic in her eyes.

She wanted to erase him.

Everyone rushing to comfort me with the hope of a future in which Thad's memory faded, they wanted him superseded, not because he had become for me a source of great pain, but because he was ultimately expendable, an empty space waiting to be populated by some other child. Widows and widowers did this, I thought, remarrying while their spouses decomposed in the dirt. Six feet above their humiliated corpse, the person they had loved most in life lay on their marriage bed, looking into the eyes of some new lover, grateful for them, fucking them with blood running through their veins. You are as ultimately meaningless as your worst fears would have you believe in your darkest moment, and worse, you will be replaced, erased, and the world moves on, happy for new things.

I thought of myself as a conscious skeleton streaked in the brown muck of decayed flesh while Leland walked down the aisle with some worthy Southern bride, his family celebrating this great feat of redemption. He'd compare her to me, grateful (and maybe guilty) for all the things she readily offered that I was unable to give. They would speak of me fondly, on appropriate occasions, recalling trivial quirks to pay respects without the unnecessary inconvenience of truly remembering. On nights when this fantasy tormented me, I would ask Leland, "If I died, would you find someone else?" And he would patronize me. "How could I?" a sugary non-answer, but I would accept it as a numbing agent and go to sleep.

My dad wasn't there to wrap the horror of it all in his particular brand of pseudo-sage bullshit. Three months after Thad was born, my father came down with the flu. Predictably suspicious of the money-hungry medical establishment, he'd denied my mother's pleas to visit the emergency room even after he'd begun to hallucinate and soil himself. Anger crowded my ability to pity him, and I encouraged my mother to leave him on their living room couch, shivering under an old blanket, his creased forehead beaded with sweat.

"What can I do?" she'd ask, not wanting an answer, not really.

"Nothing, Mother," I'd patronize, sarcastic. "You're so helpless. No action can be taken. No action of any kind."

"You know how he is, Tessie."

"Totally. There's nothing that can be done."

Upstairs, I could hear the plodding footsteps of Peyton in her lithium daze, oblivious to her own world as it shriveled on the vine, like a rotting apple, brown and mealy in her mouth.

Before Peyton was sick, our mother would call us with meaningless updates. She was convinced that little occurred beyond the bubble of her petty travails with Dad, their troublesome neighbors who let their porch lights shine through the night ("It's just impolite!"), and the affairs of our extended family members ("Your Uncle Travis is separated from Linda again"). She seemed either uninterested in our lives or unable to consider them until they somehow intersected with hers in some worthwhile way—holidays, remembering a cousin's birthday, attending the wedding of a family friend.

"Why, Mom? Why would I go to Miss Janet's son's wedding?"

"Because it's the polite thing to do, Tessie."

"I haven't seen or spoken to Miss Janet in years, Mom. I don't even know her son."

"Yes, you do. He was at Marshall's graduation."

"I was in his general vicinity once. That doesn't mean I know him."

"You've known Miss Janet since you were a baby."

"We are not a meaningful part of one another's lives, Mom. It shouldn't matter to Miss Janet whether or not I attend her son's wedding."

"It's the polite thing to do, Tessie."

A week into my father's sickness, my mom nearly collapsed shouldering his weight as she walked him to the couch. He'd been casting furtive eyes about their kitchen during dinner, clearly unable to recognize his surroundings, afraid of them. My mother had to convince him he was not in a moving car. When he threw up on her tablecloth, she insisted he lay down. Calling the hospital would be impolite. Calling the hospital would just mean bad news, as it had with Peyton. Maybe if they'd never taken Peyton to the doctor, they'd never have found out something was wrong with her, and things would've stayed the way they were. Later, she'd tell me his skin was like fire that night, his pores leaking the yellowy smell of sickness. When she had him on the couch, her side soaked in his sweat, he asked about me.

"Call Tessie," he said, just once, gripping my mother's arm.

"Okay," she assured him, though she did not call me. When my mother attempted to stir him a few hours later, he was already cold. That was how she put it: "He was already cold."

Whenever I'd think about my dad after that, I'd think about this thing my mother had said—"He was already cold"—and how this made us alike. The day that Thad died, a long winter descended. I found myself wondering with some regularity if people described me as "cold." I never heard them say it, but I felt so cold, I knew they must have seen it. I had been so warm before—something said of me by friends and strangers. I'd gone cold to Leland, cold to Ouida, cold to a mocking world that refused to slow down and recognize this evil thing that had happened. Everyone wanted to move on, like none of it mattered. I was the only one left to preserve Thad somehow, and I was aware of other people in my life years prior that had since been excused from the siphon of my need. I could see then that Thad could, like these old phantoms of love and friendship, fade from my concern given time. This only aggravated the ache. It's easy in the darkness of it all to forget that I was good once, a kind woman, complicated, but full of joyful resilience and patient resolve. Before.

People often said I was "warm." Even my seminary professors, they'd say, "You're a sweet, warm gal, Tessie, you just don't know your place sometimes." My dad would mention it as a weakness: "You're too warm and naïve." Leland said it made him love me. On cold nights, he'd inch toward my side of the bed, saying, "I can always count on you to keep me warm."

• • •

Ruben asks, "Will you watch the tape?"

After a while, I answer. "Probably."

The heat changes, a stale mugginess, and my hand moves involuntarily to swat flies from my face. My throat contracts at the stale reek of garbage. Ruben and I are standing knee-deep in refuse, a veritable mountain of trash overlooking an industrial zone on the horizon, smoke billowing from candy-striped stacks. Birds hover over the wasteland, landing carefully, pecking through the avalanching debris. Mangy, scabbed dogs limp sickly amongst the rubble.

Ruben is watching a teenage girl stumbling in the distance. Her dark hair pulled in a long braid down her back, she cradles a heavy-looking shape in a turquoise wrap around her abdomen.

"Where is this?" I ask.

A heron lands several feet from where I stand. "Should you be here?" I ask it.

I can see now that the teenage girl is carrying a child, maybe two-years-old in the wrap. She slows, examines her surroundings, looking panicked, and pulls the toddler from the wrap. The child is crying now, a sincere cry, gasping for air as the teenage girl sets it down amongst the garbage and, as if the child were a ticking time bomb, the girl turns and runs, tripping, scrambling her way out of this wasteland of filth.

"We can't do anything, can we?" I ask, my voice shaking.

"No one did," Ruben says.

The baby goes on crying as its mother vanishes from sight. It cries until it sounds like it might faint from crying, then it cries some more.

This feels right, I think to myself as I drive. The passing streetlamps light the backseat, where, in the rearview mirror, I can see the reflective black scutes of Ruben's armored back. Leland's shotgun is propped against the passenger window, like a companion. My driving is stiff and uncoordinated, jerky, my reflexes dulled from inexperience. Ouida was right, I need to get out of the house, get some fresh air, stretch my legs, take things one day at a time.

I realize as I entertain this encouraging inner monologue that I am smiling. In fact, my cheeks feel sore from it. I reach up to touch my face, to confirm the smile, and then have some awkward trouble ending the smile. I laugh, a crazed snigger. I am suddenly concerned about this drive, spinning my head around to ensure I am, in fact, driving at all and confirming that yes, I am. I can't remember getting in the car, but it made perfect sense to me that I was there, like how I could never remember falling asleep but didn't really question how it happened. The isolated glow of a Waffle House catches my attention, and I pull over as if compelled by instinct.

The restaurant is empty except for a fry cook behind the counter. He watches me enter, studies me, then asks, "Aren't you cold?" his eyes on my body. I look down, realize I'm wearing only a dirt-streaked white slip and mud-caked sneakers.

"Sorry," is all I can think to say.

The cook shrugs. "Doesn't bother me."

I slide into a booth and thread the fingers of my shaking hands to steady them before me. A waitress appears with a cup of water. "You hungry?" she asks.

"I think so," I answer, sounding like I'm trying to figure something out.

"Be right back."

As the waitress vanishes, the cook goes on staring at

me, then asks, "You know who you look like?"

I furrow my brow and shake my head, no.

"That gal from *Footloose.* The one who dances with Kevin Bacon."

I nod and smile, make a patronizing grunt of a fake laugh. When the waitress returns, I ask her if I can order alcohol.

"No, sweetie, we don't serve alcohol. Do you want some sweet tea?"

"Yes."

"Looks like you took a bad fall."

"What?"

She points to my bandages.

"These are alligator bites," I say. She laughs.

I nod, looking away, and the waitress eventually abandons the conversation, likely thinking me high or insane. When she's gone, I examine my body. To anyone looking, I'd seem as if this is the first time I've occupied a foreign vessel. I pull my collar away from chest and look down my slip. The voice of the cook startles me from my examination. "Everything look okay down there?" he asks with a lecherous wink.

"No," I answer, looking away.

• • •

MY DAD HAD A sister no one talked about. I think that it was one reason my parents were so ashamed of Peyton's "problem." This mysterious aunt of mine was some kind of alcoholic or junkie, with an embarrassing succession of husbands and children—uncles and cousins we'd never met. Peyton and I pieced together a spotty record of her—a shameful phantom—with dozens of overheard phone calls and arguments between our parents. Then, one afternoon when I was eight, we went to her house. I'd been terrified when the school principal interrupted our class in the middle of the day to announce that my father had arrived to pick me up, something that had never happened before. The principal walked me to the school office, where we found my father waiting with Peyton, anxiously pinching his chin, staring at something only he could see.

He loaded Peyton and me into the passenger side of his pickup truck without a word, and only after we'd been driving for ten minutes did I muster the courage to ask what was going on.

"We have to drive to your Aunt Sarah's house," he said without looking away from the windshield.

Her name a baleful omen spoken aloud, like cancer, Peyton and I wheeled around to face one another in panicked surprise.

"Why are we coming with you?" I asked.

"Because your mama was out, and I couldn't get her on the phone."

"Why did we leave school early?"

"I didn't know how long I'd be."

"Did something bad happen?" Peyton asked, afraid.

"I don't know," he lied.

We drove southeast to Richmond Hill, beyond any sense of civilization there, and down a winding dirt road, limbs of reaching trees whipping the truck as it went. Pulling into a lonely driveway, overgrown with sun-bleached brambles, my dad parked the truck in front of a dilapidated-looking house with a rusted tin roof. He climbed out of the cab, circled the truck, and opened the passenger door.

"C'mon now."

"We don't want to go in," I said. "We're scared."

"You ain't sittin' in the truck. It's too hot. And I don't want you wanderin' around out there gettin' into God knows what. Now don't make me tell you twice."

Peyton and I, holding hands, followed our father up a set of sagging wooden planks and over the threshold of the foreboding home. The inside of the house was oven hot, clouded with the dank must of neglect and decay. Mildew-speckled bed sheets were tacked haphazardly to cover the windows, and where they would not reach, tin foil completed their work. The whole den was suffused with a sickly lemon glow.

"Sarah," my dad shouted, something like fear or frustration or both in his voice. When no one answered, he waved for us to follow him further in, stepping over stacked dishes encrusted with hardened food and white blossoms of mold. Stacked on a table littered with beer cans and dirty laundry, a dust-caked TV played a muted episode of *The Newlywed Game.* I could see long rivulets of sweat running down the back of my dad's neck as he went, calling out to Aunt Sarah, eventually arriving in the bedroom doorway where he froze.

"Sarah," he said again.

I peered around my dad's leg to behold a claustrophobic dwelling strewn with garbage that surrounded a bare mattress on the floor. A shirtless black man was buttoning his jeans as he stepped through the junk and passed us in tense silence. The only other things in the bedroom were a sleeping woman in her underwear, and a baby's crib. My dad stomped through the mess, took the woman by her shoulder, and shook her violently.

"Sarah," he said. "Get up, goddammit."

The woman was spare except for her distended paunch, a sheen of sweat covering her exposed body, matted hair stuck to her glistening neck and forehead. I could see her struggling to lift herself from whatever deep well of stupor had bedded her down.

"Who is that?" she drawled.

My father, still shaking her, answered, "It's your brother. You called me. I didn't want the law on my doorstep by sundown if you'd gone and killed yourself."

I startled at a presence sidling up beside me and turned to see a boy, maybe five or six years old, naked except for a sagging diaper. He chewed a long, dirt-caked fingernail and said, "We're not allowed to come in here when Mama's got company."

A spasm in the nearby crib, barely perceptible, caught my attention.

"That's my baby brother," the boy said.

While Dad struggled to rouse the sluggish woman, I crept over to the crib and peered between its rails to see a sallow rat-like thing stirring within. A baby with sunken eyes and skin like latex stretched over its skeletal frame was lying on a pad layered with what looked like days of dark, watery shit. It blinked slowly, pathetic little limbs fighting gravity like a weak puppet.

"Get away from there," my dad barked at me. To this lethargic woman, our Aunt Sarah in the flesh, he said, "You want me to call the law? Huh? Have them drag your sorry ass out of here and find God knows what and get these damn young'uns put in a home? Huh?"

The boy in the diaper said, "She's tired."

Peyton had lowered her forehead into my back, wanting to disappear.

I watched as my dad released Aunt Sarah and peered around the chaotic heap of a bedroom as if looking for something to resolve his predicament.

"Shit," he said.

A faint mewling sound came from the baby. I remember thinking it didn't look real. It looked how I imagined an alien might look.

In two big strides, my dad abandoned the room and his attempt to wake the sickly woman on the floor. Peyton and I needed no cue, we followed after him, practically running to escape the awful house.

"Are we leaving?" Peyton asked.

"Yeah," Dad answered.

"Are you calling the police, Daddy?" I asked.

"No," Dad answered.

In the doorway, I turned to take one last look at a cousin I'd never met before that day. He was still standing in his mother's doorway, the only fully conscious person in the house. With one hand, he was picking fretfully at his cracked lips, and with the other, he was waving goodbye.

3

ONCE, WHEN I WAS a little girl, my sister and I crucified a large grasshopper. In Georgia, a species called the eastern lubber grows to mammoth proportions for a grasshopper, the size of a mouse. These slow, lumbering things crowd roadside vegetation and gas station windows in the summer like an Old Testament plague. One summer afternoon, Peyton had captured a large specimen and was chasing me through the overgrown weeds of our backyard with it. I was terrified, not of the grasshopper, but of being pursued by it. Peyton had it pinched between her index finger and thumb, its segmented limbs swimming awkwardly in the air as she ran. I was older and faster, and when I'd outrun her, I threatened horrible things if she did not abandon the chase. I was almost always able to overpower her with my words.

Sniffling, Peyton leaned over, ready to return the

lubber to the brittle sunbaked grass. “Wait,” I said, freezing her. “Let’s mess with it.”

We fashioned a cross out of a broken twig using Krazy Glue, then fastened the insect to it. I felt regret almost immediately but was afraid to vocalize it. Peyton giggled, but I knew she was faking it. In a moment, I could see myself as if in a dome lined with windows, most of them fogged. The windows, I knew, were glimpses into futures that were contingent on this or that thing I did or did not do, or this or that thing someone did or did not do to me. I saw myself through one clear glass, hardened in my potential for cruelty, capable of awful things. We left the suspended grasshopper by the edge of the wood, and that night I cried myself to sleep.

I had repressed the memory of this awful thing until Thad was two. Full of wonder, he located a lubber on a gardenia in our front yard.

“Mama!” he shouted, nearly unable to contain his joy. “Mama, look how big! Mama, look!”

I was smiling as I approached, wanting to embrace him, to somehow fan the little flame of his childhood wonder, that it might burn into his adolescence and adulthood. Several feet from the gardenia tree, I could see the tar-black exoskeleton and bright red markings of the lubber, and the memory pierced my mind like an arrow fired by my past self. I was frozen for a moment before I could shake the memory, and I watched as Thad eased his small, cautious finger to the grasshopper. He seemed so timid that I wanted to reassure him.

"Don't be scared, sweetie. It won't hurt you."

"I know, Mama," he said. "I'm being careful so *I* won't hurt *it*."

Thad called Ouida "Aunt Ouida" and would tell complete strangers things like, "My Aunt Ouida has brown skin," which almost always evoked confused non-responses from the recipients of this information. Other people, even other parents, often seemed stilted and phony when interacting with children that weren't theirs. They put on cartoon voices, hammed up exaggerated responses to simple things, talked to Leland and me through Thad: "I bet your mama is so proud!" or "You sure look like your daddy!"

Ouida and Lucius were unable to have children, and

Ouida loved Thad the moment she first held him in the delivery room. Other visitors pretended to gush over him, put on a big show, likely exhausting themselves from the presentation, but when first offered Thad, Ouida received him gratefully and cried quietly to herself while she rocked him.

Unlike the other adults to come and go from his life, Ouida's presence extended beyond the hazy margins of Thad's memory. She had been as familiar and benign to Thad as the sound of his own voice. Ouida felt perfectly comfortable correcting Thad, and Thad felt perfectly comfortable defying her. Leland couldn't understand why their occasional skirmishes brought me such joy. Embarrassed, he would urge me to step in, and laughing, I would ask why. Unable to pronounce R's, Thad would declare, "Don't talk with me anymow, Aunt Ouida!" and without hesitation, she would fire back, "Oh, I'm going to talk with you as long as it takes for you to listen, you can count on that!"

The day he died, I stepped over a precipice. I knew what I was doing. For a moment, Ouida followed. She held me on my bathroom floor, sobbing, she slept on my couch, and I could hear her crying through the night. Ouida's husband, Lucius, a man with whom I had never been able to connect, appeared in the whirlwind of it all. He stood in my living room, wringing the hat he had dutifully removed upon entrance, unable to meet my gaze. He didn't apologize for "my loss," and he didn't promise to pray. He sniffed back tears and told me, "I sure will miss him."

In that moment, Lucius wasn't just another spectator in the coliseum of my agony, he came to contribute his own, and I loved him then.

Mornings were the waking nightmare. A short drift in the solidity of consciousness so sweet and so cruel that, for a moment, Thad was still alive, still in his bedroom sleeping. Then, like a frightened deer, the mirage would turn and flee and the world itself would wither in its wake, paint peeling from the walls, flowers wilting, fruit shriveled and fuzzed with white, swollen with maggots.

The more I concentrated on recalling specific sensations from my stockpile of memory, the more my connection to them faded. Images of Thad became drugs to which I was developing a tolerance, and they no longer seemed as if they belonged to me at all but were as alien to my own life as an old movie I'd once seen or a story I'd heard from someone else. I studied pictures until they were abstracted, just a random organization of shapes and colors. Jeffrey, my boss, came to check on me weeks after it happened, and I overheard him in the other room talking to Leland in a controlled whisper.

"When my mama passed, the best thing for me was to just stay busy. Hell, Leland, that was a woman I'd known for more than forty years, and even then, I didn't carry on like this."

His words, I remember, permeated my hardening shell of detachment and found the old me—the warm me—somewhere inside. I was a little girl, and Jeffrey's words were a great glowing moth that hovered over me, and with blunt but necessary clarity, invited me back out through the hole it had made to get in. The moment was so lucid that I remember thinking, why this? Why these simple, stupid fucking words when so many other smarter, better people had said and done things with infinitely more compassion and eloquence? Jeffrey, a sad, stupid man—the kind of man always assuming he knew more and better, despite knowing nothing—had just blathered these unfeeling, ridiculous words, and here they were, a shining spirit animal prepared to lift me from the dark well of my despondency. And to my great surprise, I was ready to leave. I was ready to stand, to put one foot in front of the other. I reached up to the enormous dangling legs of the luminous moth and discovered my hand passed right through them.

I wasn't going anywhere.

• • •

I wake up in, of all places, my bed. I sit up, realizing I'm naked and look around, confused. Daylight floods the bedroom from the drawn shades, and the room itself is in total disarray. The TV is blasting from the living room. I turn to face the alarm clock on the nightstand, but I'm immediately distracted by an image taped to the wall: a poster print of Gustave Doré's *The Destruction of Leviathan.* Doré's wood engraving depicts a roiling ocean where a colossal sea dragon flees before a robed, sword-wielding image of God, who parts the clouds above the monster.

In seminary, I'd written a paper on the text that inspired this illustration, having spent hours staring at it hanging on a classroom wall. I was nearing graduation, and the professor graded the paper favorably. He was a small, sweet man, one of very few who seemed wholly uninterested in me being the only woman in his class, treating me like any other student. I received this as simultaneously refreshing and frustrating that in overlooking my uniqueness, he also overlooked my plight. When he returned the essay to me, he extended a rolled parchment bound by a rubber band, and smiling, said, "Excellent work, Tessie." I unrolled it later, in private, revealing the Doré print that had inspired the essay. Fixed to the print was a note that read, "I'm sorry that seminary was often an unforgiving place for you, Tessie. May the Lord empower you to slay your own dragons as you go from this season of life to the next. Blessings."

Sitting up in bed, my body glistening with sweat, the heater making the house feel like a stale oven, I stare at the print, blinking. I lick my cracked lips and speak aloud the text on which Dorē based his work:

"In that day, Yahweh will punish with his sword. His fierce, great and powerful sword. Leviathan the gliding serpent, Leviathan the coiling serpent; he will slay the monster of the sea."

When someone knocks on the front door, Ruben stirs on the carpet beneath the bed. "Be quiet," I say to him. I crawl around on my mattress, surveying the room. I seem to have haphazardly emptied my dresser drawers—along with the secret contents of my closet—all over the floor. Socks, Leland's underwear, a few bras, and newspaper clippings detailing child death litter the carpet where an ancient-looking black reptile sits, cold and heavy and motionless.

The knocking on the door becomes incessant.

Leaping over Ruben and through the open bedroom door, I manage to find an afghan draped over the arm of the couch and wrap it around my naked frame like a shawl. The TV is playing an ad for Folgers Coffee Singles at an absurd volume. I crack the front door to end the knocking and find Ouida looking afraid and confused on the front step.

"Is this giving me space, Ouida?" I ask, peering through the crack like an agoraphobic.

"For God's sake, calm down, Tessie. I just stopped to see if you need anything on my way to work."

"I'm fine."

She reaches out and applies gentle pressure to the door, eyeing me apprehensively. "Why don't you have any clothes on?"

"I fell asleep with the heater running, and I got hot."

She nods her head as if this seems reasonable. "You don't need anything?"

"No."

"Have you talked to Leland yet?"

"Not yet. I will."

She nods again, like a doctor taking notes. "You look crazy."

"I need coffee."

She takes a step back, sighing. "Get some rest," she says before turning to her car, the engine still running.

I rush to the TV to end the horrible racket and find an unlabeled VHS loaded into the open VCR.

"Are you going to watch it?" Ruben's voice asks from behind me.

"Do I have to do it right now?"

"We don't have much time left."

"I know."

• • •

When the Darkness settled in, Ouida worried that I would lose my faith. Everyone was talking about God then, but Ouida was defending him.

"He's mysterious," she would say, her arm around me. "We don't know why he saw fit to take Thad home now, but we have to trust him."

"God didn't *take Thad home*," I said.

"You're hurting. I know you are."

"He didn't do it, Ouida. It was just this stupid, random, horrible thing. Not some ridiculous divine scheme."

Ouida squirmed, screwing up her face at my blasphemy.

"If anyone had some mysterious reason in mind behind all this," I went on, "it was the devil."

I remember saying the word *devil* and imagining some cartoon imp in red pajamas, but there in my mind, the fiery goblin became Doré's winding sea serpent. I watched as the watery dragon wound itself up from the depths and on to dry land, wet dirt sticking to its armored hide. The Charlie Daniels Band soundtracked the scene in my mind.

The devil went down to Georgia

He was lookin' for a soul to steal
He was in a bind
'Cause he was way behind
And he was willin' to make a deal

In my imagination, stubby legs grew from the bubbling sides of the dragon as the steaming primordial swamp grew arching oaks from its bog, Spanish moss reaching down from their branches overhead as the devil hissed and bellowed, now fully transformed into a hungry alligator.

• • •

In the scattered debris of the bedroom, I discover an unopened box of condoms. A momentary surge turns my stomach before recognition sets in, a wave of warm relief. These were the condoms Leland and I had always used, though this box seems undisturbed. It dawns on me then that the box was likely purchased before Thad died, when Leland and I were still having sex, and that neither of us realized the purchase would prove pointless. Standing in the bedroom, holding the box, it occurs to me that if I could have seen Thad's death on a timeline, so many purchases and plans would have been rendered obsolete: the swimming lessons later that summer and the new swimming trunks to replace the ones he'd outgrown, a Godzilla action figure I found in a clearance bin and was keeping for his next birthday, a single can of SpaghettiOs.

This seemed different, the box of condoms. It wasn't a swimming class with a dead boy's name on the roster, it was a totem of something else I had no idea was doomed. Unlike other young, new parents, Leland and I never struggled to maintain passion for one another. We returned to one another's bodies like wells of sustaining life force. Other moms would search me for solidarity, saying, "I just want to warn these newlyweds to take their time because they don't realize they won't be going crazy once the little ones come along." I would smile and nod, unable to relate. Thinking about it now, I can't remember our final moment of intimacy, and this feels like a new kind of loss. I open the box and examine a foil-wrapped latex coin. I remember seeing one for the first time in the sock drawer of a friend's older brother when I was about twelve. I was scared of it then. I slammed the drawer and fled the room, panting. I had no idea how familiar, how functional these artifacts would become, like a bar of soap or glass for water.

I feel an overwhelming desire for Leland—for his arms and his comfort and the smell of his skin. I allow myself a brief fantasy: Leland returning, confessing he had failed to comprehend the validity of my pain, but that he was prepared to walk with me through the fire and out the other side. I collapse into him, my rigid exterior melting away until I am nothing but tender, exposed flesh, and he lets me cry into his chest, and maybe I would start to snap back into place somehow.

When the daydream concludes, I examine the devastated bedroom and realize this is not a realistic backdrop for such a fantasy. I sort through a pile of clothes, some of which I've vomited on at some point, and find a relatively clean and wrinkle-free summer dress with a blue floral pattern. It suddenly seems critical that I drive to work.

The drive to my office creates a strange sense of isolation. There are no cars or pedestrians, the sky an even slate of grey. I'm distracted by a worming paranoia that the world has been evacuated without me. When I finally arrive at work, the familiar parked cars give off a sense of relief, and I rush to the door. When I step inside, I become immediately aware of myself as a foreign presence, a virus, offensive to behold.

Someone says my name like it's a question, drawing the gaze of everyone in earshot. Someone else flees the room, shuffling awkwardly. Jeffrey, my boss, appears before me like a wraith, a barrier to keep me from further infecting the clinical sacredness of the room.

"Tessie," he says. "What can we do for you?"

I roll my eyes, attempt a natural laugh that instead comes out canned and psychotic. "You work for me now? It's about time!"

He inches in. "Why don't we get some fresh air."

"It's cold out there, Jeffrey."

He looks at my dress. "You wanna borrow my jacket?"

"So chivalrous."

"Let's go outside."

He opens the door for me, positioning himself in such a way as to funnel me out of it. Outside, my skin is goose-bumped and pink, my breath steaming through my chattering teeth.

"Jesus, Tessie. You're freezing."

"I like the cold," I say, rubbing my arms.

"Leland told me you were taking the rest of the week off." He eyes my bandages, furrowing his brow. "Said you had an accident."

I hold my arm up to examine it like it's the first time I've ever realized I had an arm in the first place. It doesn't look good. The wound has seeped through the bandage, creating a cloudy brown Rorschach pattern with accents of leaking yellows. I say, "Oh shit," when I see it, but then recover gracefully with a chuckle, adding, "It looks worse than it is."

"Do you want to wait in my office while I call Leland to come pick you up? I know he wouldn't mind."

I am now desperate to end this interaction, this moment. "If you guys don't need me today, I'll probably just head back. Come in on Monday."

Jeffrey scans the parking lot, then looks back to me. "Let me just call Leland. He'll take you home. Change those bandages for you."

I laugh, fanning the air as if to dispel this suggestion. "I just talked to him," I lie. "Don't worry about it. I'll just see you on Monday, Jeffrey."

I can see now this venture was a mistake. It seems inevitable that Jeffrey will call Leland and describe our encounter with stupid, hyperbolic hysteria. I am aware of an evaporating timeline as I speed recklessly back to the house.

. . .

In the way of social interactions post-Darkness, this was far from the worst of it. In August, Leland dragged me to a neighbor's cookout. The patio was festooned with faded patriotic garlands clearly arranged for the 4th of July and left to bleach in the sun. My cheeks ached from the effort of a wholly inauthentic and unconvincing smile.

"You look like a robot would look if a human tried to teach it to smile," Ouida told me, drinking from a red plastic cup.

One by one, those in attendance approached me as if the area around me were a funeral, and by entering into it, they must assume funeral voices, tilt their heads, raise their eyebrows, refer to both themselves and me as "we" at all times. "How are we doing?" and "Well, we sure are praying for you."

"Who?" I would ask.

"Who?" they'd echo back.

"How is who doing? Me and you?"

"You and Leland."

"That would be, 'How are you doing,' not, 'How are we doing.'"

I could overhear conversations about me and couldn't tell if I were paranoid or perceptive. It was like a voiceover narrating the barbeque. "She doesn't look good," and "She just needs to put one foot in front of the other," and "Leland seems to be handling it a lot better than she is."

No one understood that I needed to feel this. I wasn't wallowing or refusing to "get better." There was a strong current, and I needed to see where it was taking me, though no one else was willing to come with me.

I was having a problem with water then. When I looked at it, I always saw it clouding with blood. It didn't seem like a hallucination. It felt like closing your eyes after being blinded by a bright light only to see exploding orbs beneath your eyelids. I'd look down at the water in my red cup, never drinking from it, and I'd see a blossoming red plume contaminate it. Sometimes I convinced myself it was the light permeating the red plastic. Other times I knew it was no illusion, there was blood in the water.

• • •

The porches in our neighborhood are all lit with crude jack-o-lanterns. My feet are freezing in the dead brambles of grass, and the barrel of the shotgun makes a scraping sound as I drag it along the road beside me. A year ago, Thad decided he wanted to go as a Tyrannosaurus for Halloween. Unsatisfied with the crude, ill-fitting costumes on offer at Savannah's department stores and costume shops, I'd decided to sew one together myself. Thad thought the costumes depicting smiling, cartoonish dinosaurs were "too silly," and that he wanted to be a "scary" T. rex with "big, sharp teeth."

Four-year-old children are typically dressed for Halloween to amuse their parents and not themselves. Parents wanted to see adorable costumes, not scary ones. But I badly wanted to satisfy Thad's desire, so I fashioned for him a more realistic disguise from fabric, cardboard, and papier-mâché. Other parents offered vocal admiration of my work, assuming it had been done for that very purpose, but when Thad first donned the disguise, lowered his brows, wrinkled his nose, and snarled at me, disappearing into the costume, I was completely compensated for my efforts.

What is it about dinosaurs and reptiles and fanged monsters that so wooed the imagination of children, I wonder as I stand shivering, gripping the butt of the shotgun? Why do they draw them, play with toys, read picture books, ask to dress in Halloween costumes?

I can see silhouettes gathering in a window or two, likely staring at my strange and troubling presence, standing in the middle of the road dragging a firearm. I look behind me and see my parked car on the highway's shoulder, the driver door open, behind it, a purple soup of twilight.

I feel vulnerable like this. Putting Ruben in the car (an idea that seemed crucial hours prior) feels like a mistake. I take a deep breath and watch as it becomes wisp of grey fingers in the air then vanishes. I am becoming increasingly aware of some imminent catharsis. My behavior over the last couple of days becomes imbued with purpose. I am nearing a destination. The world slows down—nearly stops—and I know whatever is waiting for me is at home, not here.

• • •

A few years ago, a horrible incident at a small waterpark off the Georgia coast made international headlines. The articles all claimed that a small boy had been killed on a waterslide, and that another adult passenger had suffered a fractured skull, but none of the articles described what had actually happened or why. I remember, at the time, thinking it better not to know. After Thad died, the incident resurfaced in my memory, and I was briefly consumed with the quest for answers. After a week or two of lunch breaks spent sorting through microfilm at the Savannah Library, I discovered a small article buried in a Jekyll Island newspaper peppered with the word "decapitated."

Due to a failure to uphold weight regulations, the boy was thrown from his raft as he and two other passengers plummeted down the slide's merciless drop. His head hit a metal support beam overhead and was torn from his neck before the severed head collided with the passenger behind him, breaking her jaw and fracturing her skull. Eyewitnesses described the boy's limp, headless body tumbling down the slide, dyeing the water a dark crimson as it came. I sat back in my chair before the library's glowing monitor, breathing slowly, and felt relieved that his horror was likely over in an awful flash. I wondered who retrieved the boy's head.

That evening, I asked Leland if he remembered the boy that died on Jekyll Island several years prior.

"On the waterslide?" he asked, not looking up from his dinner. He sighed and nodded. "Awful."

"He was decapitated," I say.

Leland looked at me, frustrated and incredulous. "I don't want to hear about that," was all he had to say. How, I wondered, could that be?

I prodded a string bean with my fork, *Life Goes On* playing quietly on the TV in the background. Leland assumed that because I did want to hear about it, something was wrong with me and right with him. He believed that I was obsessed with this awful thing or that I was thrilled or entertained by it. Really, I hated it so much I couldn't stand it. Not knowing seemed like another way of forgetting this boy and what had happened to him, which seemed crueler than making dinner a tad unpleasant.

When I was in fourth grade, I happened upon a book about the French Revolution in our local library. In 1905, a French criminal was beheaded by guillotine in the public square. The observing doctor wrote of the incident in detail, and I copied selections of the report and hid the notes away in my backpack. The doctor watched as the severed head was taken by a string of spasms before going slack. Then the doctor called the executed criminal's name. The doctor wrote:

"The eyelids lifted up, this time, I swear, in a distinctly normal movement, slow, as if awakening, or torn from thought. With pupils focusing themselves, the eyes looked sharp, not like a dying man's, not vague, and when the lids went shut, I called again, and again, without a twitch, they lifted, and the eyes looked into mine."

This horrible story scratched at the doors of my mind like a persistent black cat. I could not shake it. I imagined the doctor calling the dead man's name. I pictured the criminal, reduced to a head, his eyelids drifting open, shifting to the calling doctor where they focused in, then closed again. In my mind, this was like a frustrated man stirred from sleep.

After thirty seconds of this awful exchange, the head complied no longer.

I discussed this story openly only once. A classmate had invited me to Sunday school, and though my father mocked my interest in going, he did not forbid it. In Sunday school, we read about the beheading of John the Baptist. He'd made a woman mad, and when offered the world, the only thing this woman could draw from the bottomless pit of human desire was a severed head on a plate. One boy expressed confusion over this gesture of revenge, saying, "If she really wanted to get back at him, she should have had him put in a dungeon and tortured."

"Why?" a confused girl asked.

"If they just chop his head off, he's dead. He doesn't even feel anything."

I spoke up, excited, explaining what I had read in my book about the French Revolution.

"That's enough," said the teacher.

"How come so many people get their heads cut off in the Bible?" someone asked.

"It was a different time," said the teacher.

"David cuts Goliath's head off," I said.

"No, he doesn't!" someone scoffed. "He hits him with a slingshot!"

I nodded, "And then he cuts his head off with a sword."

We waited while our teacher searched for the story, visibly conflicted by our interest in the Bible's violence. When the beheading was confirmed, someone posed a subsequent question: "What did he do with Goliath's big, huge head after he chopped it off?"

Our teacher peered down at the Bible, and without looking up, answered, "He took it to Jerusalem."

The small class was, for a moment, lost in thought.

A voice came from somewhere in the group, "I sure wouldn't want someone just carrying my poor head around after they chopped it off."

• • •

I twist my ankle dragging Ruben by the tail from the backseat of my car. I'm not sure what time it is, but it's been dark for a long time. The moon is full or close to it, and my skin has begun to hurt from the cold. My floral summer dress is damp from the wet grass where I've fallen, and my bare feet are caked in black grime. Ruben comes sliding out from the car with a heavy thud and hisses in the grass, mouth wide. I run my fingers through my hair and find it tangled and oily, the grit of dirt under my nails scraping my forehead. When I look back at the house, I can see I've left the back door open, *Quantum Leap* blaring inside.

"You are wasting time," says Ruben.

"I know."

"We need to go now."

"Wait."

Ruben turns the slow, slithering way of alligators on land, inelegant and sluggish. He opens his mouth again to hiss, a low bellow droning, a harmony with the wind and insects. I realize I'm shaking. I remember hearing that dogs will sometimes eat grass to make themselves throw up, so I try it, but it doesn't work. Then the grass hardens beneath me in an instant, and I can see that I'm back in Thad's room. Gone is the frozen disorder of the last few months, the room is tidied and smells of perfumed detergent. A small, rotating globe projects a night light of planets, moons, and stars on the walls and ceiling. A few feet from where I sit, I can see myself—a past me—knelt on the ground beside Thad's bed, where he lays on his side, smiling up at this other mom, her face untouched by madness and despair.

Ruben's cold, scaly side slides against my thigh, and I put my face in my hands, trying to remember to breathe.

"Why aren't you looking?" Ruben asks.

Sobbing, I peel my hands away from my face with great effort, and I can see the bright blue of Thad's eyes, the smallness of his smile. Then, what I'm most bracing myself against happens, and I am undone: the sound of Thad's voice.

He says to the other me, "Mama, where does God live?"

The other me answers the way I remember answering. "Well, in the Bible, God lives in a place called 'the heavens,' which is kind of like a special place that people can't see."

He draws his knees up to his chest, his small hands

up to his chin, and asks, "Is that where Grandpa is?"

"Why would you think that?"

"Because Daddy says when someone dies, they go to heaven."

The other me leans over Thad and tells him, "In the Bible, when people who want to be with God die, they go to be with God in God's space."

"Forever?"

"No. At the end of the story, God brings everyone back here, to our world, and he makes everything in the world better so that there aren't any sad things ever again."

"What about the people who don't want to be with God?"

"They don't have to. They go somewhere else."

"Grandma said that your daddy is going to live in heaven forever and ever."

The other me nods thoughtfully. "Well, guess what? I went to a special school just to learn all about God and what the Bible says about God."

"You did?"

"I did."

"Did you draw pictures at school?"

"No, I didn't draw pictures. But one of my teachers gave me a special drawing one time."

"A drawing of what?"

"A great big dragon."

Thad's face lights up. He smiles from ear to ear, clutching his hands together in front of him. "I want to see!"

The other me pulls Thad's blankets up to his shoulders and says, "Maybe tomorrow I can show it to you."

Beside me, the current me, Ruben asks, "Did you show it to him?"

Through my sobbing, I say, "No."

The other me kisses Thad's forehead and cheeks. He giggles and reaches out to embrace me, and I hold him for what seems like a long time.

The current me, the me shivering and scraped and bandaged and covered in dirt, I ask Ruben, "Can I please go to him?"

"We're not here. Not really."

I cover my mouth again, closing my eyes, and nod.

The room changes and becomes disheveled, jarring in its contrast. Spilled Legos litter the carpet, plastic dinosaurs are strewn haphazardly, picture books mangled and torn, broken crayons and stacks of half-finished illustrations. Thad is sitting up in his bed, screaming.

"Why are you so mean?" he shrieks.

I turn to see another me in the doorway, tired-looking, wild hair in a sloppy ponytail. I level a stern finger at him and snarl through gritted teeth, "If you don't lay down in that bed and shut your mouth right this second, I am going to come back with a trash bag, and I am going to put every last toy in this room in the garbage and take it to the dump."

"No, Mama," Thad wails. "No, please…"

"Then be quiet!" the other me growls, stomping down the hallway as Thad goes on crying quietly to himself.

"Stop it," I say to Ruben.

I watch as Thad's face screws up in an awful little grimace as he clutches his pillow. His lips are moving.

"Listen," says Ruben. "He's praying. What is he saying?"

I listen for a moment. It's the twenty-third Psalm. He learned it in Sunday school.

"He's using it to pray?" Ruben asks.

"He doesn't understand it. He's just saying what he can remember."

In the bed, Thad whimpers, "The Lord is my shepherd, I lap nothing. He makes me lay down in green passers, he leads me beside quiet waters, he afreshes my soul."

"Please," I tell Ruben again. "Please stop this. Let's go."

Thad says, "Even though I walk through a darkest valley, I will fear no evils, for you are with me." He pauses, opens his eyes, and seems to search his memory for the missing pieces of the Psalm, then closes his eyes tight and continues, "Surely good things and love will follow me always of my life, amen."

"I didn't know he said that to himself," I say through shallow breaths. "I wish I could have every moment. Every single moment."

The room fades to darkness, the dull glow of light in the hallway bathing Thad in a golden haze, barely visible. His placid expression suddenly twists, and he writhes in his sleep, a nightmare entangling him.

"I need to wake him," I say. "Please."

Ruben doesn't answer.

"Thad," I try to say, my voice hoarse with tears. "Thad, baby, wake up."

He stirs, still sleeping, then convulses, whimpering, unable to shake himself from the bad dream.

"Thad, baby," I say again, thinking maybe Ruben was wrong, maybe I am here, and this is why, to wake him.

Then he does wake, the nightmare reaching fever pitch so that Thad bolts upright, his eyes open wide and staring back into me. My lungs fill with ice, my eyes welling up again. "It's okay," I say, my voice shaking. "It's okay, baby. It was a dream, just a dream. I'm here."

But Thad takes no comfort from the voice he can't hear, that isn't there, not really. He scans the room in a terrified panic, his breathing rapid and shallow. "Mama?" he whispers, barely audible. "Daddy?"

"Thad," I say, louder this time, but my voice returns void.

Thad settles back down into the bed, his eyes scanning the darkness of the room as they drift shut.

I clamor to my feet, stumbling out of Thad's bedroom door and down the hall on limbs throbbing beneath my bandages. I fling open my bedroom door to find Leland and myself sitting up in bed, watching television, images from *20/20* flickering over our dull expressions.

"Get up," I say, unable to convince myself of the pointlessness of doing so. "He needs you," I say, crying again. "Please."

Stumbling back to Thad's room, I topple headlong into a void that opens in the carpet beneath me and land in a painful crumple on what appears to be a grassy meadow. Lifting myself up on my hands and knees, I see Thad several feet before me. He's standing before a dark, humanoid shape, which gives off a sound like bundles of cracking twigs as it turns to face him.

"Wake up, honey," I call out. "It's just a dream."

The shape becomes a hunched goat standing upright on hind legs, its long, tangled hair hanging in tatters like a black robe. It towers over Thad, who quakes at the sight of it, crying, calling out for Leland and me.

"*No,*" the towering Goat says, a horrible thundering word that makes Thad cover his ears. I want to go to Thad, to put myself between the Goat and my son, to protect him, but my limbs are unresponsive, made of lead. The Goat rears up, cloven hooves paddling the empty space in front of it, as an awful mewling siren erupts from its open mouth. Thad and I cover our ears, grimacing as the Goat seems to rise and swell before us, the cloudless blue sky like a banner around it. The mewling call crescendos, unbearable, and its mouth yawns open until the stretching flesh of its jaws tears like runs in a nylon stocking. A black tendril emerges from the open maw, whipping, until the weight of whatever is on the other end breaks the lower mandible and tumbles from inside the ruined face in a wet bundle of black gore.

The fallen black growth, a horrible sodden clot in the green grass, unfurls in smooth, slithering movements, revealing a massive alligator.

Thad screams for me as the alligator lifts its belly from the ground on raised legs, making awkward, dragging steps toward him. I can see that Thad wants to run but can't move. I want to call out to him, to go to him, to stop this from happening, but I no longer feel as if I'm occupying my body at all. I can't hear or see the scene, and I'm not there, just a floating consciousness somewhere, somehow aware of this awful nightmare.

Ruben, I am thinking, Ruben, please stop this.

"The Star-Spangled Banner" shakes me from a dark limbo, and I sit up, my face stinging from the pink imprint left by the carpet. On the blaring television, a line of uniformed soldiers salutes an American flag as the final, dramatic cues of the national anthem ring out, and the image is supplanted by a horrible, ringing test pattern, then static and white noise. The static casts a flickering shaft of electric glow into the otherwise darkened living room, dancing across Ruben's scaly armor where he lies coiled in a tangle of emptied Styrofoam meat trays and some of my more expensive outfits. I don't remember getting the clothes or why I would have done such a thing, but it looks like half of my entire closet is strewn about the living room. I'm still in my blue floral summer dress, but there's a dark stain across my chest. I realize I'm still shaking and see then that the French doors are open.

Staggering drunkenly to my feet, I lumber toward the doors, nearly tripping over the shotgun haphazardly nestled in the carpet. I lock the doors then silence the television without turning it off. Ruben stirs, a slight movement, then settles again. My bandages are hanging from my arm and leg, the tape made useless from blood and sweat and the strain of whatever I've been doing. Eyeing the exposed injuries in the dull flicker of the TV, they seem darkened and swollen, glistening blood still pooling in the irregular pattern of punctures.

"Play the tape," Ruben says.

"No," I croak, my mouth dry and caked with fuzz.

I limp to the kitchen and find a pitcher of soured sweet tea. When I've finished a glass and a half, sticky rivulets running down my chin, I need to sit. Ruben enters the kitchen on raised legs, sees me, collapses on his belly, his tail seeming to unspool beside him.

"They're going to come for you," he says.

"Who?" I ask.

"Someone."

"I know."

I use the kitchen counter to pull myself up from the floor. Ruben watches what I'm sure is a ridiculous-looking ordeal without stirring. Then, when I've steadied myself on wobbling legs, he says what he always says, "We need to go."

"I don't feel like we're through yet," I say.

"We're not."

"How much is there before it's over?"

"A few more things. Not much."

My legs give, and I slide down the counter, gathering in a sloppy heap on the linoleum. "I just feel like I need to rest," I say.

"Rest is coming," he tells me.

I notice my Bible on the linoleum under a soiled napkin. I attempt to retrieve it without moving my lower body, just an animated trunk using its hands like feet that stick to and peel from the kitchen floor as if they were sneakers in a movie theater. I aggravate my injuries in the process but manage to extend my fingertips to the Bible just enough to pinch and claw it into my grip. Leaning back against the cabinet, I bend the soft binding and run my hands over the crinkled-looking faux leather cover. My name is engraved on the lower right in gold cursive. The Bible, I knew, was under my side of the bed. Something that—in a time that now seems centuries past—I reached for in the morning immediately after waking. How it got here, in the kitchen, I don't remember.

I press the tip of my thumb to the edge and fan the

thin papers. My thumb catches a bookmarked section somewhere near the end. Blinking and stretching my drying eyelids, I open the book. Tucked in chapter 11 of The Gospel According to John, is a photograph. Though its presence startles, even horrifies me, I know every detail of this photograph by heart.

It was fall, a year ago now. Thad is in Leland's arms, an expression of absolute glee on his small face. Leland is nuzzling Thad's neck, kissing him. Behind them, the church our family attended for several years until the Darkness set in. Tears flood my eyes in an instant, though I realize as I examine the photo that I'm smiling. A small laugh escapes from somewhere in me. It was a Sunday, but Leland is dressed in a red t-shirt that reads, "Enjoy Coca-Cola!" Leland was oblivious to the unspoken formal expectation of Sunday morning, and this small congregation had either not cared or else thought it in poor taste to mention. They welcomed our family, welcomed Leland in his ridiculous soda t-shirt. I, of course, knew better, but I had enough of a rebellious streak for the both of us since Leland had none.

The pastor, a towering, resilient old man that

everyone called Papa Herschel, was relaxed and disarming.

"I knew your daddy," he told me, smiling as I shook his hand for the first time. "Yes, ma'am, I sure did. He and I worked together on more than one occasion."

"You're an electrician as well?" I asked, already uncomfortable at the mention of my father.

"Was a carpenter, like the good Lord himself, though far less talented, I'm sure. Your daddy and me, we worked on a few houses together right here in Savannah. That would have been, oh, many years ago now. Before my seminary days."

Leland spoke up, surprising me. "Tessie here is a seminary graduate herself."

The pastor looked at Leland, considering this, then back at me. "Is that right?" he asked. His big, calloused hand enveloping my small soft one, he reached up and put his other hand on my shoulder. Looking me in the eyes, a big smile on his face, he said, "Well, all right then! Tessie, I don't have to tell you, but the Lord himself said to love God with all your heart, all your soul, and all your…"

I realized he was waiting for me to finish his sentence.

"Your mind," I said.

His smile widened. "That's right. And I can think of few means better suited for loving God with your mind than seminary." Releasing my hand, he stood up straight and considered me. "I bet you were in classroom after classroom full of Bible-thumping good ol' boys."

"I was."

"They chew you up and spit you out?"

"They tried."

The pastor erupted into a deep, genuine laugh. Then, looking at me again, he said, "Oh, they try, just like the devil himself. But you know, Jesus crushed that old snake's head. You keep up the good work, Miss Tessie." Turning to Thad, who was hoisted up on Leland's hip, the pastor asked, "Is Mama tough?"

Smiling and shy, Thad nodded.

"Damn right," said the pastor.

And though I was cautious, I liked him already.

Papa Herschel—like several others from the church—had called, knocked on our door, spoke to me through Leland when I refused to see him. One by one, all of them gave up except for Papa Herschel, who continued to call on Monday mornings. Sometimes Leland answered him, sometimes I think he couldn't bear the work of putting a positive-sounding spin on the same, tired update: things are still bad.

I think about all of this holding the photograph, but not for long. What I'm really thinking about is the way things come undone and how sometimes that's a good thing. Here was my husband, Leland, breaking a generational curse of affectionless fathers by unabashedly kissing his son. Here was Thad, who had only ever known a father who kissed him. I should have given up on God and on church by then, the way my father had done, the way my classmates had expected, but there we were.

It strikes me, the way that we observe photographs as images of memory. I was there, there I am. Pinching this thin, paper thing between my fingers, I remember taking the photo. I was laughing. It was a warmer autumn, not as miserable as this one. I remember feeling so overcome by love that it was almost devastating. I remember thinking, if only for the briefest moment, how truly and horribly fragile all of this could be.

Now I know.

Before I tuck the photo back into the Bible, I can see where I've underlined John 11:35 and what I've written in the margins beside it.

Jesus shed tears.

• • •

WHEN I WAS IN third grade, a poor girl in my class happened upon her mother's dead body. I don't know why children form alliances, separate the weak from the strong, pick them apart, leave them to die. Mackenzie Bauer was quiet and skittish. Her clothes were ill-fitting and faded with time, her hair a blunt bowl-shaped mop obviously sculpted by an amateur. There were rings of dirt in the creases of her neck.

Mackenzie's mom retrieved her from school every afternoon. A pear-shaped woman with oversized, insectoid glasses and long, straight hair pulled back to accent her tall, glistening forehead. I never saw them speak to one another. Mackenzie would move dutifully to her mother's side before the two of them would drift silently to the school's exit.

The other children loved to marvel at Mackenzie's unwillingness to engage when under attack. They'd loop their little fingers through holes in her threadbare dresses and ask, "Why don't you get new clothes? Are you poor?" They'd comment on her house—a sad, algae-covered shanty all of us neighborhood kids knew well. "Why don't your mama never cut your grass? How come your house is turning green on the outside?" Practically catatonic in moments like these, Mackenzie would stare forward, vacant, and I wondered if she was like a turtle withdrawing into its shell, waiting for the predator to give up and abandon its prey.

Little boys would write Mackenzie love letters, satires, hoping to coax her from the turtle shell long enough to tear her apart, but she could not be coaxed. They would hand them to her at recess, and she would not take them, and the boys would hate her all the more. I remember feeling heroic when I attempted to broach conversation with Mackenzie, but she refused to participate, likely suspecting a trap. I hated her then. Here I was doing her a tremendous service, a benevolent act of charity, and she had the nerve to reject it. I remember thinking if she would just yield, she wouldn't have to creep through grade school like a skittering rat.

One week, Mackenzie didn't come to school at all. I hadn't really noticed until my mother asked me about her.

"Do you know a girl named Mackenzie Bauer?"

"Yes, ma'am."

"Did you know her mama died?"

I puzzled at this, not knowing what to make of it, if I was being tested. I shook my head, no.

"Awful," my mom said, I guess, to no one. "Just awful."

That night after dinner, I lingered in the hallway while my parents watched reruns of *Lancer* and I overhead the awful fate of Mackenzie's mother.

"...Her daughter is in Tessie's class," my mom was saying to my dad. "Tessie didn't know anything about it. I don't reckon she'll be back at school for a spell."

"How'd she go about it?" my dad asked.

"A shotgun," Mom answered, lowering her voice. "Angie said she was out there for two days before her little girl found her. The two of them lived all alone in that old house down there on Magnolia. Poor thing got so scared she finally went out lookin' for her mama. By the time she found her out back, the ants and possums had already got to her."

"She'd been out there that long?"

"Angie said the doctors think it didn't work at first."

"What didn't work?"

"It's just awful."

"What didn't work?"

"Angie said she might have shot wrong."

"Shot wrong?"

"So that she didn't pass right away."

"Jesus Christ."

"She might have been out there for hours like that."

"I don't know how in the hell you survive a shotgun blast."

"I can't bear to imagine it."

"Damn shame that little gal didn't wander back there sooner."

"I wish she hadn't wandered back there at all."

I thought about Mackenzie for days, wondering what she saw. I imagined her mother sprawled out in the weeds of their backyard, her face an explosion of gore, her lifeless body ransacked by animals and insects. I imagined her mother's final hours, blind and sputtering, gasping for air through the wet ruins of her opened skull. I wondered why Mackenzie didn't call for help in what must have been the terrifying days she spent alone before finding her mother's corpse. I wondered who she finally called after she'd found the body. I wondered if she'd ever come back to school.

She didn't.

Many years later, in 1986, Leland and I watched a boy on the news who had tried unsuccessfully to kill himself with a shotgun. His parents would later claim he was being manipulated by subliminal messages in a heavy metal record. We had been married for a year or so, and Leland was perplexed when I crumbled at the sight of this boy, weeping. His face was a puckering twist of waxy flesh set beneath two eyes, a drooling marionette jaw gibbering his marble-mouthed story. Leland thought I was scared of this mangled face on the TV. I told him about Mackenzie Bauer, how little concern I'd shown for her.

He said, "Sweetie, you were a little kid. You didn't know any better."

But that's just something you say. We both knew I did.

2

THE NEXT MORNING THINGS get worse. When I wake up, the grey daylight of October has filled the kitchen. My back aches from where a kitchen cabinet handle was wedged between my vertebrae. My neck is stiff, feels compressed. When I move my legs, they feel like they're breaking free from clay casings. Out of the kitchen window, I can see Ouida and Leland getting out of Leland's work truck. Leland approaches the work shed while Ouida waits, her arms crossed, eyes on the house. I can't tell if she sees me.

Gripping the countertop, I survey the kitchen. It's not good: a congealing brown lake from a spilled tea pitcher. A stale refrigerator smell. Limping to the living room, my injuries are all fire and ache, *Designing Women* is playing silently on the TV, the French doors are open and filling the den with a frigid breeze that stirs the emptied Styrofoam meat trays and my strewn lingerie and formalwear.

By the time I step outside, I realize that though I thought to don Leland's flannel bathrobe, I didn't bother putting on shoes, which is, of course, the first thing Ouida notices.

"Tessie," she says, already pointing at my feet as I approach. "You're going to catch a cold walking around on this cold grass barefoot."

"You don't catch colds from cold feet, Ouida," I say without stopping. "Colds are viruses."

Leland emerges from the work shed. "Don't come over here," he says to either of us, I guess, though neither one of us is moving in his direction. "Something happened to Luther."

"The dog?" Ouida asks. "What do you mean something happened to him?"

Leland fans the air away from his face as if warding off a smell. "Something got to him. Bigger animal."

"Something got to him?" Ouida echoes. "In your shed?"

Leland closes the shed and locks it like he doesn't trust us to leave it alone.

"What are you guys doing?" I ask.

They both look up at me as if I've said something ridiculous.

"We came to check in on you," Ouida says. "Why were the doors open."

"I just got back from a walk," I lie.

"You went for a walk in a bathrobe?"

"No. I changed."

Ouida makes a disbelieving *mm-hm*.

Leland, it seems, can't bear the sight of me.

"Let's go inside," Ouida says. Leland looks at me for…what? Permission?

"I was just about to clean up. It's a mess in there. I've just been vegging out and napping, mostly."

"Oh, please," Ouida says dismissively. "Tessie, you know no one cares about any of that nonsense."

"Ouida," Leland interjects, nodding with his brow furrowed. "Let's give her the space she wanted." I can't tell if this is meant to honor or hurt me.

Ouida rolls her eyes and throws her hands up in exasperation. "Tessie, I'm about sick of all this nervous breakdown shit."

"Ouida," says Leland, a warning tone in his voice.

"No, Leland. She's gonna hear about it. Now I know

the whole world has gone to hell, but you're not going with it. We've cried, and we've hurt, and we've looked the devil right in his ugly face, but I'll be damned if I'm going to look at it forever and I'll be damned if I'm going to sit here and let you do it either. So fine, clean up the house, get dressed, do whatever it is you need to do, but you better believe me when I say I'm coming back and we're going to talk about how the hell you're going to get on with your life."

"Ouida," Leland says again, louder this time. I look at him and realize he's not looking at Ouida, but at the house. I turn in time to see Ruben's heavy black tail disappearing from sight as he crawls in and out of the visibility afforded by the open French doors. I whirl back around to face Leland, and he's already moving toward the house.

"Leland," I say, panicking. "Leland, listen."

"What?" Ouida is saying. "What happened?"

Startling both of them, I challenge Leland's heavy stride with an explosive hobbling sprint, Leland's robe peeling from my body in the breeze as I go. Then he's running behind me, and I can hear him saying "Tess" like this is more delicate than screaming. Like this helps.

When I cross the threshold, I trip over the shotgun, twisting my ankle, falling on my throbbing arm. Reflexively, I reach for the gun, and then Leland is standing over me, the ash-sky in the open doors making him a threatening silhouette. Like a character in a movie, he's showing me the palms of his hands, a "slow down" gesture, still saying my name but nothing else.

A guttural bellow sounds from behind me, Ruben uncoiling, hissing, showing the two of us the pale pink insides of his mouth.

"Leland, wait," I say, my voice shaking, and he staggers backward, just barely, and I realize he's afraid. Ouida is behind him now, panting, furious, saying, "Look at yourself, Tessie," and "For God's sake, Tessie." I'm biting my lip, eyes closed, hugging the cold shotgun, and I say, "Just stop it, everyone stop it," but they can't hear me over Ouida's hysterics, so I scream it.

A moment of quiet passes; Ruben's hiss the only audible thing. *Designing Women* has become *Family Feud.* I attempt standing, fumbling with the gun as I rise like a newborn fawn.

"Christ almighty," Ouida says, pacing dramatically.

"Out here in October in that little dress, looking like she hasn't bathed in a month, looking like she survived a car wreck, grabbing hold of a gun like she's lost her goddamn mind."

"Tess," Leland says, but his eyes aren't on me. He's scanning the living room, taking it in. I can see all his notions of me, his wife, eroding as he beholds this thing I've become, and I can't stand it. I think for just a second that what I really want is to somehow escape my own body, like a specter erupting from a shell, and leave this scene forever. But I'm stuck here. My ghost will not be willed from its fleshly bonds.

Leland advances, his arm out and hand open. For a moment, I think he intends to seize me, but then it occurs to me he means to snatch the shotgun from his deranged wife, so I stagger backward and evade him. He pursues a few paces but then freezes when I feel my heels meet the cold, soft leather of Ruben's flesh. I look down and see the alligator wreathing my ankles, a half-moon, his hissing jaws fixed on Leland.

"Tess, come here," Leland says. He's frozen, not wanting to agitate the animal, afraid it will attack me. But I know Ruben won't kill me. Not yet, anyway. We aren't finished.

"I just want a little space," I say. "Just a little bit more time to think," and I step backward over Ruben so that he's in front of me now like a rabid guard dog. Leland and Ouida are, I can tell, stunned. They watch as I attempt to pull Ruben backward by the tail into Thad's room before I discover I'm too weak, my wounds inflamed from running.

"I'm going to call someone," Ouida says, her voice shaking.

"Stop it, Ouida," Leland says, and I grip the shotgun, furious. He's *embarrassed*, I realize. Don't call someone. I don't want anyone to know about my wife's insanity. It isn't polite.

"I just want to be alone for a little while longer," I say, affecting calm.

"Tessie," says Leland, "you're going to hurt yourself."

Hurting myself has in no way occurred to me until this moment, and his panic at the idea seems powerful.

"I won't if you leave."

"Get away from it," he says, meaning, presumably, the alligator. I take another step backward.

"Now go."

"I'm calling Lucius, and you two can get that thing out of here," Ouida says to Leland, like I'm not even here, her voice like air escaping a tire.

"Dammit, Ouida," Leland says, but never adds anything to it.

I feel like an idiot. I feel like someone who has fallen face-first in shit on her way to a wedding but goes anyway.

"I'm going to move it," Leland says, his eyes on Ruben.

"Don't!" I shout. "Please, Leland." But he's ignoring me, making a sweeping creep around the living room in order to sidle up beside Ruben's tail undetected. I'm not brandishing the shotgun, just hugging it. I wonder if I should point it at something, but I feel self-conscious about it.

"Leave it alone, Leland," I say. "You'll get hurt."

As Leland closes in, I step one foot over Ruben so that I'm standing over him, straddling him. Something ignites in my arm, an explosion of pain, and I only realize Ruben has bitten me as he's pulling me to the ground.

"Ruben," I gasp.

Ruben rolls once, and my body reflexively attempts to turn with him, but he's faster and heavier and the bones in my forearm snap, sounding like a string of exploding fireworks. My vision dulls, my body reacting mechanically, struggling, and I can hear Ouida screaming, and I see Leland inches away, his hands on Ruben's jaws as he grunts and wrestles, and I think about Thad.

Ruben rolls again, and there's a hot, tearing sensation, electricity surging up my arm and into my chest and head and the tension releases, then I'm falling and skittering backward like an injured spider. Leland is over me now. I'm drifting, and sleepily deduce that I must have been placed in a warm bath, but no, I'm moving, and I realize Leland is carrying me, my side warm and soaking wet. I think someone is pouring warm water on me, but when I look to see who it is, I see that I'm covered in blood, my blue dress turned black and red. I also see that my arm is wrong, turned backward somehow. There are ragged ribbons of flesh curling back around the angry tangle of meat that was previously my elbow. I can see the dull, pearl gleam of bone, some pinkish and purple-looking tubes, snapped and protruding from the gushing disaster. Leland's shirt is turning black and with my good arm—the one I can move—I reach up and flatten my palm on his chest as he cradles me like a child, and I think he's running but to where I don't know.

. . .

Thad loved dinosaurs and prehistoric reptiles, snakes and insects, things with sharp teeth. I used to watch him with his toys, organizing and enjoying the plastic wildlife and rubber grasshoppers, overlooking the little trucks and bulldozers and green soldiers he'd been given for birthdays and Christmas.

When he turned four, Leland brought home a handful of G.I. Joe figurines in their boxes and eagerly fanned them out before Thad, explaining the significance of a toy that had mattered to him as a boy. Thad happily mirrored his father's excitement, but I could tell it was his love for Leland, not for the toys. Thad examined the packages dutifully until one figure captured his full attention.

"What's that one, Thaddy?" I asked.

I was worried it would scare him, a menacing-looking brute in a black mask with glowing red eyes. The package read, "Code Name: Croc Master." The box boasted a colorful illustration of the so-called Croc Master pulling a leashed crocodile by a spiked, iron collar.

Thad settled his index finger on the animal. "It's an alligator, Mama."

Leland looked over at the toy. "I don't remember this one," he said. "That's actually a crocodile, son."

"No, Daddy, look," Thad said, smiling. "A crocodile has a skinny snout, only alligators have fat snouts." He ran his finger over the artwork. "See? Fat snout."

I could see Leland consider this, charmed by his son's expertise, and he told him, "You sure are one smart boy, Thad."

Thad smiled, radiating pride from his father's approval.

"But that fella looks like a bad guy," I observed, pointing to the figurine.

Ignoring this, Thad exclaimed, "Look! He comes with an alligator too!"

Packaged next to the action figure was a crude plastic

reptile to accompany the Croc Master. Leland peeled open the cardboard package and produced the Croc Master and his pet, both of which Thad gratefully received.

I observed Thad for the weeks that followed. The Croc Master was promptly abandoned, but the Croc Master's ostensible crocodile accompanied Thad in the bath, the backyard, the car. One night I stood undetected at his bedroom door watching as he lay in his bed, and in the glow of his nightlight, he moved the plastic animal back and forth across the mattress in a smooth winding shape, as if it was swimming. As if it were hunting.

Sometime during the plastic crocodile obsession, Leland arrived home from work one evening with a rented videocassette.

"Look, Thad!" he said, retrieving the tape from a small plastic bag. "Daddy brought home a show about alligators!"

For a half-hour, Thad was elated by what was, for Leland and me, a fairly dull nature documentary exploring the diet and life cycle of the American alligator. I had nearly fallen asleep, the narrator's droning monologue soothing me when I heard him say something about a pig.

There on the screen, a bundle of feral hogs crowded a muddy Louisiana riverbank, grunting happily as they drank from the brown water. Then, floating like a scaly black log came the dark shape of an alligator in the water. One of the younger hogs inched into the murk, looking for a less crowded spot when the enormous gator lunged from its cover and snatched the small pig by its haunches. Squealing horribly, the pig's kicking leg yawned open where the gator had bitten it, revealing a glistening pink muscle and a blooming black cloud of blood in the water. The other, older pigs joined in the squealing, agitating the waters, each of them crowding around the seized piglet, touching their noses to it, panicked. The alligator rolled the pig, its squeal broken by choking and gasping as it was dragged under the water.

I looked down at Thad, curious, and saw that he was crying.

"What's wrong, baby?" I asked him, taking him in my arms, startling Leland, who was either near sleep or lost in the documentary.

"Why didn't God help him?" Thad asked through quiet sobs.

"Who?"

"That pig."

Holding the small, fetal bundle of my son against my body, I searched my mind, my years of seminary, my impressive knowledge of the Bible for an answer that would make sense to Thad. Before I could say anything, Leland leaned over and touched Thad's head, smiling.

"Well, God made alligators too, right?" Leland asked.

"Yeah," Thad sniffled.

"Alligators have to cat to survive, right? So, if the alligator didn't eat pigs and other animals, it would die."

Thad seemed to calm.

• • •

When I wake up, I'm not sure that I'm actually awake at all. My feet are bare, toes fanning in warm white sand that stretches as far as I can see in any direction. I'm standing naked, and Ruben is on his belly in the sand next to me. My arm is still mangled, but it doesn't hurt, and it isn't bleeding. The sky above us becomes purple and nebulous, a tapestry of soaring comets and shooting stars.

"What's all this?" I ask.

Ruben doesn't answer. Over the horizon comes a distant thundering rumble, and a flash flood sweeps in over the entire sandy landscape, covering everything except the small patch of sand where Ruben and I stand, dumbfounded. Before us, the rising waters cleave, turquoise on our right, and aquamarine on our left. Out of the differentiated waters rise two radiating shapes that entangle one another. The shapes part, revealing several smaller forms in the divide, strange offspring, out of which rise a horrible, thin cry. I cover my ears. Ruben seems to squirm. The two greater shapes quiver and undulate, squirming in the awful racket.

The two great shapes twist and shift, one taking the form of an ax, the other a sledgehammer, and together they wind backward, ready to dash the shrieking child-shapes who seem to recognize the impending threat. The lesser shapes scramble like insects on to one of their parents, gnawing and tearing it to pieces as the other great shape flees into the darkness of space overhead. Alone, the small shapes regroup, seem to conference among themselves before an agreement is reached. One of the small shapes swells and hardens, growing until it towers over the others, an appointed warrior. This new warrior-shape turns upward, catapulting into the heavens in pursuit of its fleeing mother.

When the two shapes meet in the dark star-speckled canopy above us, the mother shape has become a dragon—a great, tangled jabberwocky—snarling in space, rearing back as her pursuer approaches. The serpent's offspring—now a bronze humanoid warrior—readies an arrow and takes aim. The rattling dragon strikes, fastening unhinged jaws around the warrior's skull. Before the mother dragon can consume her son, he seems to breathe deep and exhale within her throat. The monster's eyes roll back as her belly swells, her bite going slack. The warrior frees himself, takes aim with his bow, and looses an arrow through space. The scene unfolds as if underwater. The arrow, true of aim, sinks in the bloated abdomen, which bursts, an eruption of fluorescent entrails across the sky.

The beastly gore rains down, a torrential downpour,

as the enormous viscera hurtles burning to the earth like a meteor shower. The warrior son, now a towering monolith, sets down in the waters with a crack of thunder, the flashing luminescence of raining butchery heralding his return. The warrior seems to eye the aftermath of his victory thoughtfully, catching a falling rope of bowel in his assured grip. He sets to work, fashioning from the carnage a world—mountains and caves and undersea trenches and deserts and glaciers—and eventually, with careful pinching delicacy, he forms from the blood of his mother a shivering, fragile human being.

"Always struggling," Ruben says.

"What is?"

"The world."

I gesture at the scene we seem to behold like a movie. "I never believed this is how it happened. I know this story. It's the Epic of Gilgamesh. It's an ancient Mesopotamian poem about how the world came into being. I had to write a paper about it once."

"Is that why we're seeing it now?"

"Maybe. This is how I imagined it, anyway."

"Why imagine it at all?"

I shrug.

"You like this story?" Ruben asks.

"I like that it's old."

"Why?"

"We remember it. It's probably the oldest story we have that someone wrote down, and we still talk about it."

"So, this is proof."

"Yes."

"That people can last."

"Some of them."

"Will you?"

I take a deep breath, shake my head, no.

"Why?"

If I died tomorrow, the things felt for me would be like fireworks. Noteworthy, real, but only momentarily captivating and then gone. Leland would grieve, he would hurt, and then there would be someone else. He would talk about me less and less—it's only natural—and then he'd think about me less. He and his new wife would bring me up from time to time, and Leland would say only nice things about me, erasing all the details, all the real things, until I was a polished mannequin, only happy memories, and no hurt. Thank you for your service, Tessie.

"Some of you don't last," Ruben says.

"Not really anyway."

"You don't want Leland to erase you."

I take a deep breath. "I don't want him to erase Thad."

"So, there's this…" he faces forward, the poem realized in the space before us. "A story told, enduring."

"It's something," I say. "Something lasting."

"But you don't believe it?"

"I don't. I think it's stupid."

"What do you believe?"

"I'm not sure. It's hard to explain."

"What difference does it make?"

"Lots of the old creation myths follow a similar pattern," I say, surveying the evolving landscape of a primitive world. "It's a cosmos fashioned out of violence and death."

"A world forged in suffering," Ruben says.

"I guess."

"What makes what you believe any different?"

"No one dies, for one thing. In the story I've always

believed, the world isn't born from enmity or bloodshed at all."

"From what, then, is the world made?"

"Love."

"But things went bad. Still a world raining blood and shit."

"I guess it was worth the risk."

"Is that why you did it?"

I look down at Ruben. "Did what?"

"Made life."

Ruben crawls forward on green grass, my skin suddenly constricting in the sun. Two small children run laughing before me. I stumble backward. I'm in a front yard decorated for a child's birthday. A nearby foldout table adorned with wrapped gifts and curled streamers is encircled by clamoring children.

"What is this?" Ruben asks.

A small distance from the gift opening ceremony, I can see myself in the blue floral dress, kneeling in the grass before Thad. Ruben notices as well and crawls in the direction of this other me.

"I can't," I say.

"We can't leave unless you do," he tells me, and I

understand this to be true.

I shuffle forward as if approaching a cliff. I can see this other me, her brow lowered in menace, teeth clenched. Thad is whimpering.

"Stop it," the other me says. "*You* wanted to come here. If you can't be nice to your friends and stop whining, I won't take you to another birthday party ever again."

I'm startled by the gravity of this threat. I don't remember saying it.

"I want to get a present," the three-year-old Thad says.

"Well, you can't," the other me answers.

Thad cries.

"You are so selfish," the old me snarls at him.

The little boy reaches up to slap the other me, but she grabs him by the wrist, gripping it with such anger that I can see the pain on his face.

"Get in the car," the other me growls. She drags Thad past a gawking audience of his peers, saying to the hosting parent with a forced smile, "Sorry, I've got a spoiled-brat situation on my hands, so we'll have to take off early." Thad watches as the host laughs, saying,

"Oh, I've been there, believe me."

"I humiliated him," I say to Ruben as the other me locks Thad into a car seat, practically manhandling him. "He wasn't selfish. Not at all. He was just a little boy. I shouldn't have said that." I steady my body against a shuddering sob.

"Did it hurt?" Ruben asks.

"What?"

Ruben doesn't answer. I clutch my heaving chest and say "yes" anyway.

The hospital room is cold. The medicinal stink of alcohol and antibacterial cleanser hangs like a fog in the air. I blink, bleary-eyed, at a television suspended on the wall playing a muted broadcast of *The Young and the Restless*. A horrible agony burns my ruined arm. It doesn't feel as if it belongs to me at all. It's a corpse's arm fastened to a body rejecting it, begging to be freed of whatever venom must be flowing from its conjoined stump.

Leland's thumb—moving back and forth over the dried surface of my forehead like a windshield wiper—hurts in a good way. His touch has always been loving and coarse in equal measure, his hands an eroded landscape of time and work. I want to look at him, to say something, but my mind feels as if it's struggling to lift a cellar door. It has been trapped. The struggle is exhausting, a blur of drugs.

If Ruben had torn my arm away from my body and consumed it—as is often the case with alligator attacks—wildlife professionals would have killed him and recovered the homeless arm from within his belly. But my arm is still attached, so I don't know what's happened to Ruben.

Time unfolds before me like a movie I'm trying to watch but I can't manage to stay awake for more than a few minutes at a time. I am aware, at some point, of Ouida's arrival, but when I gather the wherewithal to react, she's already gone. I realize then that Leland is gone too, and I become entirely convinced that the most important thing is leaving the hospital.

Next, Ruben and I are standing in a desert. I brace myself against a hot, angry wind. We are looking at a vast hedge maze unfolding in the distance before us, the dark green of its perfect symmetry contrasting the fiery orange sand surrounding it.

"What's this?" I ask, squinting at the maze.

"This is what's left," Ruben answers.

When someone dies, the living people who orbit that death become experts in grief. Untainted by the indignity of death themselves and thus convinced of their own wisdom, they hover, sage-like, assessing the crumbling wreckage of the griever, allowing it. Beholden to something awful, omniscient, they call to the one in the pit, "It's okay to cry," they permit, but only for a season. Eventually, the season sours, and with it, the sage's patience. Then, it is no longer "healthy" to cry, no longer productive nor efficient. The sage calls out yet again, tiring of the pit and the person in it, "That's quite enough. Get out."

When the sun first set on my heart, ushering in the long Dark and the longer winter, I remember worrying about these bystanders calling out from the pit's edge. I felt like I was disappointing them. My pain had moved into me, over me, like a car barreling down an interstate too late to notice the hobbling dog, vulnerable, doomed. The car kept moving, leaving me in the road, my abdomen torn like a ruptured grocery sack, my insides a smattered stripe of produce on the pavement. The people I knew, these gracious people, suspended in the air above the glistening contents of my burst gut, patted my head, "There, there, it's okay to cry."

And I was grateful for it until I wasn't.

I'd crawled into Thad's room one night while Leland slept, drunken with agony, and even in the dark, the things I could see and smell became a black elephant sitting on my chest, mocking me, pinning me to the carpet where I heaved. I clawed at my ribs and back, long red rakes in my flesh, peeled skin gathering under my fingernails. Frenzied, I tore and thrashed against the elephant—against myself—until I managed to free myself and escape the room. When I dressed in the morning, I noticed Leland as he examined the zigzagging tracks on my skin. He never asked me what happened.

Before all this, I used to be a person who made things. I saw things in the world that seemed unique to my perspective, and I wanted them to stick to something. So, I wrote Leland love letters, my heart wrung out on little slivers of paper, left for him to find in his wallet, his truck, the bathroom mirror. I was naked in those letters, exposed. He embellished reactions at first, like a patronizing parent graciously accepting a child's flowers. But I could see behind his showmanship a real gratitude, an acceptance of my love, and I was happy for it.

Eventually, Leland could no longer affect his overproduced sentimentality and forgot to comment at all. I wrote fewer letters. Once, I assumed he had somehow overlooked the first letter I'd left him in a long time.

"No," he said, "I saw it. Didn't I say so?"

"Oh, no."

"Yeah, I saw it. Thank you for writing that."

I found the letter where I'd left it and threw it away.

Ouida worried that I'd become what I most abhorred, a sniveling, needy thing, a shell of a woman whose world could rise and fall on the approval of her man. But Ouida couldn't see that these letters were more than unrequited affection, they were pieces of me, artifacts. I'd ask Leland to speak kindly to me, and with a shrug, he assured me that though there were certainly lovely things tucked somewhere in the mysterious folds of his brain, they didn't always find their way into and out of his mouth.

He said this, and then poisoned me with his every compliment to other people, his every celebration of someone else. I knew that even before the Darkness, Leland had begun to tire of me. He endured me with the patience befitting an upright southern man, but his once wild adoration had shriveled and become toleration, then hardened to an ashy grey husk of resentment. When things in the world—things he was allowed to hate—reminded him of me, characters on television, strangers in the supermarket, characters in a friend's story, he directed the leaking bile duct of his indignation at these hapless victims. He'd call them names, verbally dismember them, decide what ought to be done to punish them. People who knew him puzzled over this. "Jesus, Leland, it's just a show, she's not real." I knew he was talking to me.

These bad things came in waves, almost hidden beneath the goodness of our lives, our family. When the Darkness came, the waves finally broke the dam, and our world was flooded. I thought of Job, chapter 38: "Who shut up the sea behind doors when it burst forth from the womb?"

In the last dream I remember, swimming the soup of painkillers, I was a little girl in the desert. I watched myself, long blonde hair, floral summer dress, little feet strapped in jelly sandals. I wore a crown of wilting tulips. The sky was a twilight gradient of mollusk purple, crowded with flickering stars and streaked with the zigzagging glow of comets.

I sat on the back of an albino alligator, enthroned on a leather saddle, clutching scarlet reigns, the supple hide groaning in my grip. The bridled reptile carried me across rolling orange dunes that seemed to steam in the gloaming. We came to a high point where I beheld the ruins of a hedge maze. Withered, skeletal brambles marked once-proud passages baked and mummified by time. A warm wind blew, and fallen leaves erupted like ash. I could see what was hidden by the maze for eons: a small cube of a hut that rose from the maze's center, carved from iridescent opal. I goaded my leviathan steed with my heels, and he lumbered on.

The ruined maze crumbled before us. We moved through it like gossamer, the alligator's pearlescent hide speckled with black dust. When at last we arrived at the opal hut, I dismounted, blinking slow, and moved into an open doorway—the only disruption of the hut's otherwise seamless surface. The air inside was thick with the smell of lamp oil and lilac. Bronze dowels crowned with dull orange flame lined a descending staircase in the center of an otherwise empty chamber. I knew what I would find below.

My fingers threaded in front of me, I skipped down the stairs, lamplight casting enormous dancing shadows on either side as I went. There came a smell of rotting meat and a dense cloud of flies as I completed the stone stairs and entered the crypt beneath the hut. Behind an iron gate rose a severed head impaled on a golden pike. The pike was lined with rubies and sapphires and engraved with the numerals XLIII, VIII, XLIV.

There was a rumble in the air—a bow dragging a cello's strings. Me as a little girl, my jellies clopping on the stone floor of the sepulcher, I moved in closer. I licked my lips, and the flies rushed to the scent of salty moisture, greedy for it. The rotting head sat slack on the pike, ribbons of green flesh hanging from its mossy skull. The yellowed eyes spasmed in their sockets as if they were each living things stirred from a deep sleep.

Silly child, the head said silently. Silly, stupid child.

I pinched nervously at my knuckles.

So troubled by the world's lies, the head said. As if you knew them at all. As if you could possibly know them. I know them. I am their father, said the Father of Lies. Silly, stupid girl. Everything grows from the soil of lies.

"I know that," I said, out loud, waving flies from my face.

You won't meet me down here, not really, said the Father of Lies. You only wander in dreams, uncommitted. You're afraid.

"I'm not afraid," the little me said, childish defensiveness in my voice. The head laughed, an awful dry cackle.

Soooo afraid! The head laughed. So terrified! Go upstairs, little girl. You won't find the purpose you're looking for down here, not with me. You want an unseen order, a plan. There is no plan. Only chaos.

"I know that," I said, lying, nervously chewing at my fingertips.

You know? What do you know? You're still looking

for it, all these years later. You still believe that if you connect every piece, you'll find the pattern. You think that if you keep inching backward, you'll finally see the entire painting! That the ugly splotches will disappear into a grand masterpiece if you could only see it. You'll shuffle backward forever. You'll walk backward until your little sandals are worn down to nothing, until your little feet bleed, until you collapse in the desert beyond the crypt and the ugly splotches will only be a bigger and uglier splotch, a canvas streaked with blood and shit. No order or purpose in any of it. And I am the painter! I am the maestro, and my symphony is dissonance. I am the painter, and my brush is deceit! Go upstairs. There's nothing down here. There's nothing anywhere.

Then I was an adult. A sad, broken woman—undone by misfortune. The sepulcher had become a sterile white corridor, and at the dead-end before me was a hideous painting. I wept over the painting, and I knew then that there was something beneath the blood and shit-streaked canvas I could never see, something vandalized and desecrated. Flies gathered on the canvas to eat and fuck and lay eggs.

I heard the reverberating click of approaching footsteps and turned to see a man approaching. Through my tears, I warned him, "Don't bother. It's been vandalized. It's so ugly."

The man persisted in his approach. "It's going to be removed," he said.

"There won't be anything there at all," I sobbed. "Just an empty wall. Nothing."

"Not nothing," the man said. "There will be something new."

Leaving the hospital at night is easy.

• • •

WITHIN THE MOSSY TANGLES of Chatham County, there rests stubborn bastions of a bygone plantation era. The locals call Savannah "The Coastal Empire," a kingdom of swamp ruled over by shadowy, tar-colored spirits. If you wander down the hardened dirt road leading away from my childhood home, you will witness a convergence of the old kingdom and the new—both of them ancient—where the brown, uneven trail meets the craggy grey asphalt of progress. My father hated that road.

"You watch, Tess," he told me one afternoon, me squinting up at him, a brooding shape silhouetted by the angry Georgia sun. "One day this here pavement road'll creep all the way back to the house." He looked up, back in the direction from whence we'd came and spit a muddy gout of tobacco. "Not all change is good change," he said, but not to me.

I followed him down the now-ominous harbinger of a paved road, flanked by weedy ditches where there sang hidden screeching insects. When we arrived at Arnim's market, he stopped outside the screen door entrance, presented a quarter pinched between his thumb and index finger.

"For candy," he said. "Don't ask me for no more'n this, and don't 'tagonize your sister with what ye get."

The stretching coils of the screen door announced our arrival, and Arnim peered over his reading glasses from behind the checkout counter, lowering a newspaper.

"How 'bout it, Ol' Boy?" Arnim said to my dad.

"Y'all doin' all right?" My dad asked, answering his question with a question, the entire exchange little more than a ritual.

I wandered past the uninteresting conversation of these two men, both of them in overalls, and took to exploring the familiar candy aisle of Arnim's store. Turning over a Bit-o-Honey bar thoughtfully, I started at the scrape of boot heels on the dirt-tracked floorboards, and Mr. Rodney, the local idiot, appeared like a leering golem around the aisle's corner. His potbelly stretching his plaid button-up, Mr. Rodney crept down the candy aisle, hands in the pockets of his jeans, until he arrived where I stood, and kneeling before me, said, "Hey there, Tessie."

"Hi."

His thin lips peeled back over his crowded, brown teeth, wiry overgrown salt-and-pepper eyebrows lifting over cracked, yellow eyes. "Gettin' you some candy?" he asked, looking at the Bit-o-Honey.

I nodded.

He chuckled, wrinkled his nose, and with a violent grunt hauled a wad of phlegm from his throat and into his mouth where he worked it for a moment before swallowing. "That's a purdy lil' dress."

I smiled.

"What d'ya say?" he asked.

"Thank you."

"Thank you, what?"

"Thank you, sir."

"Good girl," he smiled.

Not settled on the Bit-o-Honey but not wanting to speak further with Mr. Rodney, I affected calm and skipped to the checkout counter where my dad lingered in idle conversation with the store owner. Before the counter stood a rotating tower of vintage Southern postcards that I liked to spin for the simple satisfaction of the mechanism. As the tower slowed to a stop, I became drawn to a strange image: a row of black infants seated on a swamp log. Before them, an alligator rising from the water, its hungry mouth yawning open.

"Daddy, what's this say?" I asked, lifting the postcard for him to see.

"Says, 'Alligator Bait, on the Chagres River, Panama Canal.'"

"What's that mean?"

"Long time ago gator hunters used to set them black babies on ropes and drop 'em in the water to bring the gators up."

"Why?"

"They'd catch the gators and skin 'em. Sell the skin."

"The babies would die?"

Both my dad and Arnim laughed.

Ignoring the question, Arnim piped in. "Used ta be they'd use them pickaninnies for all kinda feed. Fed 'em ta hogs, gators…Hell, my daddy told me he knew an old nigger who'd go on about black babies rounded up on the old plantations. They'd dice 'em on up and chum the waters with it. Fish bait."

"Tessie don't need to know about all that," my dad said.

Arnim shrugged. "I don't reckon it's any worse than what they likely to teach her at the schoolhouse."

I turned the card over, revealing a passage of text. "What's this say?"

Arnim answered, "That there's an old song." He reached for the card and, pushing the glasses up his nose, read the lyrics:

Someone am a-comin' thro' de gate;

Go to sleep, don't yo' peep,

Listen to me tell yo',

Yo's mammy little alligator bait

Arnim flipped the card as if in search of further lyrics, then grunted and handed the postcard back to me.

"You like it?" my father asked, gesturing to the postcard in my hands. "Ain't nothin' but a nickel if you want to bring it home."

I shook my head. "No, sir."

He shrugged. "Put it back then."

Outside, I asked my dad what was wrong with Mr.

Rodney.

"He's just a harmless old retard. Lives in that trailer over yonder, right next to the store."

"Why does he live next to the store?"

"He's Arnim's kin. Mr. Arnim looks after 'em."

"Because he's a retard?"

"Watch yer mouth," my dad said, stern edge in his voice. "Don't you want to go ahead and open that candy on up?"

The image of the infants lining the log in my mind, I told him not yet.

"Don't you tease yer sister with it."

"Yes, sir."

"Otherwise, I might have to feed *you* to a gator."

I looked up at my father, startled, and he winked, beads of sweat already gathering on his nose like flies on some dead thing.

1

IN THE OSCILLATING UNPREDICTABILITY of Georgia weather, the frigid October has been interrupted by a strange warmth. The asphalt outside of the hospital feels balmy beneath my bare feet. A breeze stirs my hospital gown, reminding me of my nakedness beneath, and everything about the night and the weather and even my body feels somehow exactly right.

I'm aware of something coming to an end.

I'm being called to my home—as if the quaint little structure that has known such love and such agony has become a living, breathing thing—a place where I have been held and known and fucked, a container for the swirling mixture of my best and worst self. I wonder then if God can see me, and I realize that I believe he can and does. I see myself as a little girl in the arms of Jesus.

I'm still here. There's more.

Ruben has something I need before I'm done.

Alligators slow down as the weather cools. They dig out dens in the banks of cold rivers and await the sun, the season of feeding. I rove a long Savannah highway at an unknown hour of darkness, imagining the sheer volume of them, their proximity. When Thad died, I was determined to emphasize the cruelty of the event, reading about these animals, wanting to discover there was only one in all of Georgia and that this horrible thing had found us somehow. Instead, I learned that there were maybe a quarter-million alligators in Georgia, and I think of them now, a congregation of dragons, each of them waiting for a thaw.

A few cars pass, none of them stopping. I remember years before, completing the ritual of preparation, my face swathed with foundation, full lips painted red, eyes lined in inky black. I remember straightening my back before my bedroom mirror, rising like a nymph, the shape of my body lithe and curving. I could never say so, but I knew I was beautiful, that other people thought so as well. I remember Leland's eyes when we met, darting up and down my body, lingering on my chest, thinking this escaped my notice.

I imagine myself in that old bedroom now, erecting myself before the same mirror, a skeletal hobgoblin twisted by despair.

• • •

There are photographers who pose mourning parents with their stillborn babies. I learned this visiting the home of a boy Thad had befriended in school for a playdate. I sat on a couch next to this boy's mother and made small talk, the obligatory connections of motherhood. Observing a framed portrait of a man and a woman cradling a newborn, I asked if the photo was of Thad's new friend.

"No, that's his little sister," the woman told me, strange, stoic formality in her voice.

"Is she not home?" I asked, scanning the living room for signs of a second child.

"She was delivered stillborn," the woman said, her words like an anchor landing in the center of the room. She breathed in and looked away, remembering. "I had a condition called pre-eclampsia. My feet swelled all up, and I had horrible headaches, but I didn't know any better so I didn't bother saying much about it until I couldn't feel her moving anymore."

Her hand moved to her stomach. "I was about 32 weeks along. They told me she didn't have a heartbeat, so I delivered her just like that."

Wiping tears from the corner of her eye, she sighed and continued. "Can you believe they even make tiny little coffins for stillborn babies? Kasey's was pink. Had her name on it and everything. A little angel too." She pinched the air to indicate the angel's smallness.

"I didn't know that," was all I could think to say.

"Yeah. The hospital told us there were people that could come in and take some pictures so we could have something, since we wouldn't be bringing a baby home like we thought we were."

She stood and moved to a nearby cupboard, retrieving a small photo album. "They did a really good job," she said.

She extended the album to me, and I took it. The pages were filled with images like the one in the frame: black-and-white, artfully staged, both parents with serene expressions as they cradled a baby that moments ago, I believed to be living and now knew to be dead.

When I arrived at the final page, a different photo fell from the album and into my lap.

"Oh," the woman said. "Sorry, I don't like that one. My husband took it."

This other photo, crude and amateurish, looked nothing like the others. In it, the woman clutched a pale body to her chest, her face a twisted mask of agony as she bathed her daughter in her tears.

Before I left it, the hospital soothed me. I hadn't spent much time in and out of hospitals in my life, my only significant experience of one being Thad's birth. There was an annotation in the file cabinet of my memory: hospitals are the birthplaces of love, though I knew they were, for many, houses for death.

We'd been rushed from one room to another that day years ago. Leland was made to sleep on a hilariously unaccommodating cot, both of us greedy to hold Thad, a squirming pink lump who had already changed everything and for whom the future was a bright frontier of possibility. New parents, I would later learn, are often perplexed by this fragile new thing to enter their lives. When the baby slept especially still, we would lower our worried ear over his bassinet to listen for signs of breathing. We gently placed our palms on his little chest to assure ourselves of a steady pulse.

I watched Thad running with his friend that afternoon while I held the photo of the stillborn baby, and I remember thinking how grateful I was.

• • •

My house is asleep, visibly darkened and empty from the outside when I hobble across the front lawn, the fire in my mauled arm now burning through the fog of painkillers. The front door is unlocked, the living room still stinking and filthy. Everything is as I last remember it, and a conflicting sensation of both disappointment and relief moves over me like a cresting wave. I know there is now only one place where I can find Ruben. I approach the television, moving my trembling good hand to the VCR perched above it and open the loading tray where an unlabeled black VHS awaits, radiating.

I close the tray, power the machine, press play. Taking a few strides backward to keep myself from stopping the tape, I nearly faint from the effort. The tape begins where it left off, a group of children gathering at the edge of a pond, squinting into a disposable camera. I can see myself standing between the tee-ball team and the water's edge where a boy, smaller than the others, leans out over the bank, curious.

My legs tremble before I collapse, my arm exploding with pain. I'm gasping now, barely able to breathe when I see something now that I did not see then: a shape moving in the water.

Then I'm back in the desert with Ruben, the vast hedge maze extending out into the distance, farther than I can see. I know the maze is all that's left, and without speaking to Ruben, I pass through the entrance and find myself inside the tape, standing between the tee-ball team and the muddy bank of the pond. I brace myself, staggering, and turn to the water.

Thad is there, kneeling over the edge, his bright, shining face alive with curious joy, his blonde hair tousled by the summer breeze. I'm walking to him, wanting him in the picture, not wanting him to miss this moment. That I am so close to him, so very close, my breath catches in my chest. Something drifts in the pond. A log? And in an instant, the alligator springs from the water, its open jaws snapping shut on Thad's head with a wet thud. I'm in the water now, an arm around Thad, another beating the alligator's snout. Thad's face, sideways in the animal's bite, is a terrified grimace, blood running into his panicked eyes as he coughs and chokes, bobbing in the water. I'm screaming, saying something, I don't know what, desperate. Thad's little arms flail in the brown water, he pants, gasping for air as the alligator begins to pull him from my grasp. "Mama," he's sputtering, so scared, "Mama, Mama, Mama…" Other people are rushing into the water now. The alligator rolls, tearing Thad away from me and swims backward, my son still struggling as he sinks beneath the water's surface.

There are hands on me, arms looping around me, pulling me back, and it seems as if the world itself and everything in it is tearing my son away from me.

The Chatham County Sheriff's Office sent divers and boat crews armed with rifles and harpoons, roaming the waters into the night, all of them looking for something no one wanted to find. Sometime after 1 a.m., an alligator was discovered pushing Thad's body through the water. Alligators do this, I later learned, to keep their food from other predators when the prey is too big to swallow whole. A shotgun was fired at the alligator, but it escaped beneath the black water, abandoning Thad, his little face upturned to the moon. When they pulled him from the water, pieces of him were missing. Several of the searchers, I was told, broke down in tears at the sight of him.

When pressed by the media, the man who first discovered Thad said only, "I was out there all night. I don't want to talk." I read those words over and over again, and I think I loved that man for saying them. Other people, witnesses and officials, only parroted hackneyed condolences, "Our hearts go out to the family in their time of grief." One officer said, "This is a difficult time for everyone, but at least the family has their son back."

What a stupid fucking thing to say.

The tape is little more than the shaking, grainy image of chaos as something mostly obscured by crowding bystanders thrashes in the water and screaming onlookers shout stupid things like "What is that?" and "Oh no." The footage ends with a dark shape disappearing into the water as men drag me from the scene, and disembodied voices say, "Oh God. Oh my God."

Then comes a scramble of white noise, morphing into an old football game. I look around the living room, calm, taking easy breaths. The shotgun is still there in the carpet, a ghost of my last struggle with Leland. I sit there, tired, my arm hurting, imagining what it would be like to shoot myself. I try to imagine my once beautiful face as a mangled cyclone of twisted flesh and scar tissue as I drool on the evening news, pretending to be happy that I survived this horrible momentary lapse in judgment.

My head feels warm and dizzy. For a moment, it's almost like I'm dreaming. I can feel Leland's arms around me, holding me the way he did when he carried me. I'm reaching up to his face to touch the tears I see there, wanting to feel them and know they are really there, and when my fingertips are wet, I know in my heart that Leland's love for me and for Thad is complete, that I couldn't understand it before.

I can see that all of Leland's transgressions were things I beheld through a glass clouded by Darkness and were not as they seemed. He cries as he holds me, heavy in his way.

It was absurd then to imagine what I had most feared: that we didn't matter. Everything in the universe was so infused with meaning that I was being crushed by the great purpose of it all, and the pain I feel from it was something like love as Leland carries me someplace that doesn't hurt so bad all the time, and God is not distant or aloof, and he is not the cruel architect of awful things, but he becomes the one holding me, and Leland's tears are his.

And the dream slips away.

I stand, unsteady, and lurch toward Thad's bedroom, aware that I am on the brink of losing consciousness. Once inside, I lie on his bed, gathering his small blankets in my hands, and I breathe him in.

"Jesus shed tears," I say to Thad.

• • •

FROM THE TIME HE was very new all the way to the very last night he slept in our house, I would slip silently across the creaking floorboards into Thad's bedroom and watch him, if not for a moment, while he slept, and I would pray. I remember thinking of consciousness—awareness—as a house being built inside us. It starts very small, embryonic, hardly enough room to sit up, and that's okay, but then we build and expand. Soon there's a den, a second bedroom, a second floor, a cellar. We make more space for love and joy and knowledge and also fear and sadness and suffering. If the house grows, it attracts suffering, calls out to it, a cosmic beacon across the universe.

If suffering comes, it can sweep through every room and into every nook and cranny, in and out of every socket and air duct. I remember thinking about this in the orange glow of Thad's nightlight, grateful that whatever pain he'd known had so little space to navigate, and I prayed against it.

The day Thad died, I laid down my theory about the house of suffering. He was four years old; he didn't know how to tie his shoes or about loss or unrequited love, and with his head caught in the jaws of some thoughtless, hungry thing, his eyes were locked on mine, and I saw then a suffering that was absolute. But there was an evening before he was gone when Thad interrupted his bedtime lullaby to ask if, one day, he would die. My heart broke over the question, so I did not answer it.

"Why would you ask a thing like that?" is what I said. I realize now that I deflected Thad's question for my sake and not his. When the fever dream of that awful week was complete—on the night of the seventh day—I dreamt of that last day our family would ever spend at the beach. I watched the memories as film reels, and as I watched, I cried, but it wasn't the Darkness that brought the tears; it was joy. It crashed over me in waves, incapacitating me, my heart on the verge of bursting from it all, and I was warm again. Then I was in the film, embodying the memory, and I could see through the eyes of my old self, looking down at Thad's sand-speckled face, his cheeks already kissed by the sun. "This is the best day I ever had, Mama."

I saw everything as if it were drifting from me, peacefully, and the scene became my grandfather's painting. Three figures on a beach. The war was over.

Another October, I sat in a familiar park on a cold afternoon and watched the children scramble up the metal latticework, chasing each other through the felled orange foliage.

A boy that looked like Thad approached the upright xylophone, lifted the hanging mallet, and with thoughtful precision, hammered each cylinder one at a time, a sweet-sounding scale hovering in the air above the boy and the instrument. I said to a woman sitting next to me on the park bench, "I remember that xylophone sounding awful."

"It did," she said. "So many parents complained about it that they got rid of the old one and replaced it with one that has only harmonious keys. Apparently, no matter how they hit it, the notes sound nice together."

"Oh," I said.

The woman took a deep breath. "Out with the old, in with the new."

The little boy who had played the xylophone approached me, smiling.

"Did you hear that?"

"Yes," I told him, familiar hurt burning in my chest. "It was perfect."

The words are like a heavy stone rolled from a tomb, for I now speak the terrible language of life and death.

AKNOWLEDGEMENTS

Thank you to Abigail Porter, Michael Dumont, Matt Hughes, Gavin Bennett, Patrick Porter, Margret McBride, Faye Atchison, Jimmy Callaway, and Dave and Keana Zoradi.

REJECT

Printed in the USA
CPSIA information can be obtained
at www.ICGtesting.com
CBHW010246090924
14063CB00006B/7

9 798989 203833